His mouth cut her off, his kiss a hard slant of his lips over hers.

The shock of his action threw her off stride. She placed her hands on his chest, intending to push him away. Then he softened the kiss, stealing her ability to think. She sank against him, opening her mouth under his.

In the next instant she was teetering on her own feet while he strode to lean against the mantel.

Not trusting her legs to hold her, she perched on the bench of his weight equipment. She glared at him. "That was unprofessional. We're in a professional relationship. It would complicate things unnecessarily to inject a personal element into the situation."

She blinked up into his silver gaze....

Dear Reader

I had great a time writing this book. Because my love of family is so strong I bring a little of my family into every book. I'm blessed to have twin nieces, so writing about twins was fun. And, yes, they *have* traded places—but I'm assured it was harmless fun. Yeah, let's not tell their mom… And, no, they are *not* allowed to be partners in board games. There truly is something in twins having a psychic link. All kidding aside, they are beautiful young women and I'm very proud of them.

I also enjoy creating spectacular events. I think I might have a bit of a suppressed designer in me. And when it comes to Christmas tree-decorating the themed trees are courtesy of my mother. We've done it for years and have had some awesome trees. Give it a try some time!

I hope you enjoy getting to know Garrett as much as I did. I always fall in love with my heroes—we'll call it a perk—but Garrett really got to me, with his dark and brooding ways. I wish you joy in his journey to love.

Happy reading!

Teresa Carpenter

HER BOSS BY ARRANGEMENT

BY
TERESA CARPENTER

First published in Great Britain 2014
by Mills & Boon, an imprint of Harlequin (UK) Limited,
Eton House, 18-24 Paradise Road, Richmond, Surrey TW9 1SR

© 2014 Teresa Carpenter

ISBN: 978-0-263-24299-7

Harlequin (UK) Limited's policy is to use papers that are natural,
renewable and recyclable products and made from wood grown in
sustainable forests. The logging and manufacturing processes conform
to the legal environmental regulations of the country of origin.

Printed and bound in Great Britain
by CPI Antony Rowe, Chippenham, Wiltshire

Teresa Carpenter believes in the power of unconditional love, and that there's no better place to find it than between the pages of a romance novel. Reading is a passion for Teresa—a passion that led to a calling. She began writing more than twenty years ago, and marks the sale of her first book as one of her happiest memories. Teresa gives back to her craft by volunteering her time to Romance Writers of America on a local and national level.

A fifth generation Californian, she lives in San Diego, within miles of her extensive family, and knows that with their help she can accomplish anything. She takes particular joy and pride in her nieces and nephews, who are all bright, fit, shining stars of the future. If she's not at a family event you'll usually find her at home—reading, writing, or playing with her adopted Chihuahua, Jefe.

Rcent books by Teresa Carpenter:

STOLEN KISS FROM A PRINCE
THE MAKING OF A PRINCESS
BABY UNDER THE CHRISTMAS TREE
THE SHERIFF'S DOORSTEP BABY
THE PLAYBOY'S GIFT
SHERIFF NEEDS A NANNY
THE BOSS'S SURPRISE SON

Branch : Cornhill Library
Date : 23/05/2017 Time: 12:44
Name : Vinothraj, Laksana
ID : D1151653600000

ITEM(S) BORROWED   DUE DATE

Her boss by arrangement   ~~20 June 2017~~
B0000000128630   14 July

Total loans: 1
Total reservations: 0

Please retain this receipt and return
   items before the due date.

THANK YOU FOR USING
ABERDEEN CITY LIBRARIES
03000 200293

CHAPTER ONE

"Parking, code blue." Tori Randall heard the request for assistance from the valet station through her headset. They usually had three valets for an event of this size but one of their regulars had called in sick at the last minute, leaving them shorthanded. They were one short in the kitchen, as well. The darn flu was killing them.

"En route," she responded and caught her twin sister's gaze across the open expanse of the living room from where she stood just outside on the top level of the terraced patio. Lauren nodded subtly, indicating she'd heard.

"Hey, do you see the spark between those two?" Tori gestured to a stunt coordinator and a production assistant seated on the patio, chairs pulled close so their heads nearly touched. "Love is blossoming."

Lauren's gaze touched the couple and Tori knew her twin felt it, too, the sense of knowing when two people were meant to be. It was a talent they shared.

"No meddling," Lauren cautioned, though her eyes softened. She was a sucker for true love. For everyone but herself. "We agreed to focus on the business."

"We don't meddle," Tori protested. "We introduce. I don't think we're needed in any case."

"No," Lauren agreed. "They've found each other all on their own."

"The buffet has been refreshed and new appetizers are circulating." Tori gave Lauren an update on the food. This was their first event for one of Hollywood's top directors, Ray Donovan. Everything needed to be perfect. "We're past the witching hour, so desserts are coming out in a half hour. I can use a bit of fresh air."

"Keep an eye out for Garrett Black," Lauren said.

"Are you still expecting him to show? Give it up, Lauren, he's not coming. As usual." The new head of Obsidian Studios was the newest "it" guy everyone wanted at their event. But the man was refusing to play. No surprise. He had a rep for being antisocial as a director and producer. Why should running the show make any difference?

Their company, By Arrangement, had landed a coveted contract with Obsidian Studios to organize their events at the Hollywood Hills Film Festival starting in six weeks. Lauren hoped for an opportunity for them to introduce themselves to the top dog.

"Midnight is young by Hollywood standards. My source said he was planning to attend. He and Donovan go back."

"Right." Tori rolled her eyes. But the truth was Lauren's infamous sources were uncannily correct. "I'll keep a lookout."

She still doubted they'd see the elusive Black tonight. Injured in the car accident that killed his father eleven months ago and left him as head of the fifth biggest studio in Hollywood, Garrett had been conducting business from his Santa Barbara home. Until a month ago. Gossip now had him appearing at the studio daily.

She stepped outside and breathed in the salt-tinged air. Malibu was one of her favorite places in the world. She scanned the driveway filled with world-class vehicles. All was quiet. She continued down the front steps to the valet station.

"Hey, Matt, what's the problem?" She rubbed her bare arms. The fresh ocean air was heavenly but a bit crisp in early November and the black dress she'd chosen for tonight had a halter neck, leaving her arms bare to the elements.

"Sorry, Boss, I need a quick restroom break and John is taking a car down to the church." The driveway and garage held a good number of vehicles, but for the overflow they'd made arrangements to use a church parking lot down the hill.

Matt had been out with the flu last week and looked a little pale. "Are you feeling okay?"

"Yeah, just not pushing my luck right now."

Shivering, she nodded. "No problem. I'll cover. Go ahead."

"Thanks. It's slowed down a lot so maybe no one will come along." He shrugged out of his jacket and handed it to her. "Here. I'll try to be quick." And he ran up the drive and around back to the service entrance.

She shrugged into the jacket, which was oversize but not too bad, Matt being on the smaller side. Crossing her arms, she rocked on her three-inch heels, deciding in that moment to allow the valets to use stools. What she wouldn't give to sit for a minute.

With no one around she slipped out of her black pumps. What Lauren didn't know wouldn't hurt her. Against Tori's protests, Lauren demanded they wear the punishing shoes for evening events. Of course Lauren wore the spiked torture devices for hours without flinching.

Tori flexed her sore toes. She preferred no shoes at all. The cold of the stone step felt good.

The rumble of a powerful engine filled the night and a Maserati Spider turned into the drive. Tori forgot all about shoes as the beautiful machine pulled to a stop in front of her. She clasped her hands behind her back to keep from rubbing them together at the prospect of driving the Italian muscle car.

"Thank you, sir." Focused on the car, she paid little attention to the driver until he refused to release the keys, and then she looked up into pale gray eyes ripe with irritation.

He looked familiar but she couldn't quite place him. When he'd stepped out of the car, he'd turned so his features were shadowed. He wore an ill-fitting black suit over a black sweater. And from the little she saw, he didn't look in the mood to party. His square jaw was clenched, his fine features drawn into harsh lines.

One thing for certain, this guy was no wannabe, not with this car, and it bothered her that she couldn't bring a name to mind.

He towered over her, a belated reminder she'd forgotten to put her shoes back on. When she wore the thee-inch heels, it made her five-seven, but even at that height, he'd top her by several inches.

She smiled all the brighter, hoping he wouldn't notice. She tugged on the keys. "I'll take good care of your vehicle, sir."

The brooding gaze he ran over her disabused her of that notion. She had the feeling he missed little. "What do you drive?" he demanded in a gruff voice.

Now that was just rude. "A Mustang 500GT."

"Huh," he grunted but still held possession of the keys. "Is there a male attendant?"

"In the restroom." She took delight in informing him.

"Be polite," Lauren warned in her ear.

His thin lips took a downward turn. "Park it close by," he ordered as if he knew of her longing to put the car through its paces on the downhill trip to the church. "I won't be long."

The keys dropped into her palm and she nearly danced on her pink-tipped toes. She half expected him to inspect the car so he'd know if she added any dings to his beauty. But then he probably didn't have to.

She moved into the V of the open door.

"Miss." She glanced up at him. He'd stopped halfway up the steps to pick up her shoes. "I prefer you to use these."

"Of course." Skipping up the wide steps, she reached his side and accepted the black pumps shoved at her. She bent and placed them on the ground, putting her headset on Mute as she did so. "Thank you. Let's just keep this part between the two of us."

"Worried for your job?" he mocked, his lack of sympathy obvious. Up close he took her breath away. Well-defined features and shadowed eyes were framed by a square jaw and broad brow. Too masculine to be pretty, he was a beautiful man.

"Worse, a lecture." She teetered a bit and a suit-clad elbow was thrust at her. She shot him an appreciative glance that did nothing to soften his stern demeanor and used his arm to steady her as she slipped into the heels.

Hard muscles flexed under her fingers, triggering a feminine response, which flat-out annoyed her. She refused to be attracted to a jerk. Ignoring her protesting toes, she released him as soon as she had her feet encased in leather. Flipping her blond ponytail over her shoulder, she reengaged her headset.

"Enjoy your party, sir." She gave him another bright smile and turned back to the car, tugging Matt's jacket down around her hips as she went.

In the car she adjusted the seat. The interior smelled delicious, of rich leather, linseed oil and a hint of spicy cologne that must belong to Mr. Rude. She turned over the motor and it purred like a lion. She bit her lip, half tempted to take the beast down the hill after all. But she reigned in her impulsive side and pulled the lovely car into an open slot in the garage. Penance for being seen without her shoes.

Not that Lauren would see it that way.

When Tori reached the front of the house, both Matt and John were there. She gave Matt his jacket and the keys to the Maserati, told him where it was parked and made her way inside.

Lauren was waiting for her. "You went off-line. What was the problem?"

"Really?" Tori tapped her headset. "It must be a short." She gave a quick look around but her brooding combatant was nowhere to be seen. "Did you see a big guy in an oversize suit come in?" She'd hoped for a better view of him in the light to help her place him.

At least that was her story and she was sticking to it.

"No. You shouldn't lie, Tori. You're not good at it. What did he want you to use?" Lauren's honey-brown eyes, identical to her own, narrowed. "Tell me you didn't take off your shoes."

"I didn't take off my shoes."

Her sister's hands went to her hips. "We talked about this."

"And as long as you require me to wear these stilts, we'll be talking about it again."

"It's unprofessional."

"No one was around," she protested.

"Except for the big guy in the oversize suit."

"Who drives a Maserati." She couldn't hide her awe. "OMG, Lauren, it's the sweetest thing I've ever driven. I lost my head for a few minutes." She confessed.

Lauren drew her down the hall toward the kitchen and away from the crowded front room. "I suppose you already tagged Dad."

"I may have texted him a picture."

"Tori, this is an important event. We can't afford for anything to go wrong."

"Relax, Lauren. The event is already a success." Two waitresses passed them carrying trays of delectable sweets. "There go the desserts. After I put out the candy table, it's all smooth sailing." Hoping to avoid further lecturing, she swung toward the kitchen.

"Black drives a Maserati."

Surprise spun Tori back around. "What?"

"Garrett Black. Drives. A. Maserati."

"Well, fudge sticks." With the name, the familiarity fell into place. Garrett Black. She'd been thrown off because he'd cut his hair and lost weight, which explained the over-sized suit. Of course the shadows hadn't helped. "We may want to put off the introductions to another time."

"Garrett, my friend, you made it." Ray Donovan broke away from a small group near the terrace and met Garrett halfway across the room. They shook hands and Ray pulled Garrett into a full body hug.

"You threatened to pull your next movie if I didn't." Resigned, he squeezed back and then stepped away, creating the distance he preferred. "I'm no fool."

Ray laughed. "You're all kinds of a fool, but you're not stupid."

Garrett shrugged. There was no arguing with the truth.

"Let's get you some food." Ray led him to the dining room and the table spread with a diverse array of dishes, pretty, elegant dishes that probably appealed to the many starlets drifting about.

"I'm not really hungry."

"My friend, you've got to eat, you're wasting away. Get your nose out of the air. Just because food is beautiful doesn't mean it should be dismissed. This is the best food I've ever had at a party. Try the bacon-wrapped meatballs and the chipped beef poofs. I particularly like the spaghetti stuffed garlic bites." He tossed a bite-size nugget into his mouth.

"So I lost some weight. I had a broken jaw if you'll remember." Along with a crushed left leg and shattered collarbone. All compliments of an SUV crashing broadside into the car he was traveling in. He'd lived through it. His father hadn't.

Garrett felt a pinch at his lack of grief.

"Some? That suit is hanging on you, buddy."

Garrett glanced down. "So?"

"So, you're the head of the studio now. You need to dress the part. Here—" Ray picked up the plate of spaghetti bites, tossed on a few mushroom caps and assorted other items "—let's take this upstairs and you can tell me how you're doing. Oh, whoa." An attendant walked by with a plate of chocolate cupcakes. "Diane, be a doll and give that plate to my friend, would you."

"Yes, sir, Mr. Donovan." The attendant handed Garrett the plate with a smile.

Ray took his booty and walked around the corner to a spiral staircase that took them to a loft overlooking the living area below. A wall of windows offered a spectacular vista of the ocean during the day. Tonight the view consisted of the dancing on the patio below. A four-foot-high glass balcony wall ran the length of the loft.

Garrett sat down in a cream leather armchair and set the plate down on a black glass table. Ray set the food on the ottoman and Garrett took a chipped beef poof. Kudos to Ray. The food was the best he'd had since the accident. He reached for another.

"How's the leg?" Ray asked.

"Better. Therapist says it's at 90 percent."

"Wow, that's great." Ray went to the bar. "You were

pretty messed up when I visited you in the hospital. So they put a pin in?"

"Several. Total reconstruction of my thigh and knee." Four surgeries kept him in and out of the hospital for eight months. It's only during the past two months he'd felt like he got his feet under him again. "Just call me Robo Director."

"Robo CEO. You're head of the studio now."

"There's something I never expected." He accepted a Scotch, took a small sip, and set the cup down. He was driving and on meds. He'd come too far in physical rehabilitation to risk a setback now. "I have to admit I'm still wrapping my mind around the fact."

"Really? You used to have a lot of ideas of what you'd do when you got the reins." Ray dropped into the ivory bucket chair next to him.

"Not since Dad and I had a falling-out. I told you about that."

"Sure, he insisted you take on director of creativity for the studio and then overturned most of your decisions."

"I warned him to stop, but he did it once too often and I quit. He retaliated by blackballing me from the studio."

"Ah. You didn't tell me that."

"Sorry. It wasn't something I wanted to get around." Just as he didn't tell his friend about the studio's damaged reputation. "Needless to say, I figured I was out of the will."

But he'd been wrong. Or more likely Dad hadn't gotten around to changing his will in the past six years. He still didn't know what prompted the invitation to Thanksgiving dinner. Either way Garrett had his work cut out for him if he wanted to bring the studio back to its former glory. Gossip traveled fast and far in the movie business, which accounted for the loss of contracts. He didn't want anyone knowing a continuing decline could put Obsidian Studios in financial distress.

"You're an only child," Ray pointed out. "The studio has been family owned for ninety years. Obviously in the end blood was stronger thangrudges."

"I suppose." Whatever the reason, the studio was now his, and Garrett refused to let it fail on his watch.

Looking for a diversion, he swung the chair around to overlook the crowd below. Absently he reached for another meatball. Immediately he spied the sleek ponytail of his bothersome valet. She stood in a hall just off the entry talking to another woman.

She'd lost her jacket and under it she wore a halter sheath dress square at the neck and ending a few inches above her knees. The little black dress at its classic best. It didn't cling but draped her lithe figure, hinting at more than it revealed unlike so many of the other dresses shrink-wrapped on the women roaming the room.

His gaze returned to the women in black. He frowned and blinked. Then blinked again, wondering if the one sip of alcohol was enough to have him seeing double. No, there were two of them. The second woman's dress was scoop-necked and she wore her hair in a lower tail clipped back rather than banded.

"Who are the dynamic duo?" He lifted his chin in the direction of the girls and Ray shifted in his chair to see who he referenced.

"Ah." His friend's blue eyes lighted on the women with unerring precision. "They are Lauren and Tori Randall, my event coordinators. They handled the premiere of *Pretty Little Witches* a few months ago."

A dark brow lifted at that. Even cooped up convalescing, he'd heard of the successful event.

"The movie flopped," Ray went on. "But people are still talking about the premiere. When I decided to throw a party, I had my assistant call them. The name of their company is By Arrangement."

Garrett's mouth quirked up at the clever name, a nice play on their being twins. Actually the name sounded familiar. Probably in connection with the premiere. The women broke up, his valet heading to the kitchen, the other moving off in the other direction. Garrett turned away. The woman had already taken up too much of his time.

He nailed Ray with a pointed stare. "When are you going to be finished with my house?" He'd rented his place to Ray for his current film project *Gates of Peril* while he stayed at the family manor adjacent to the studio. The drive was easier on his leg, but he'd like to get away from it on the weekends. "I'm getting tired of the dusty old manor."

"Not much longer. Maybe a month."

"A month? What the hell, Ray? I happen to know you're also over budget."

"Yeah, but the special effects are sick. Another month and two million should see a wrap." The director shook his head. "The set is a circus. All kinds of people underfoot. Jenna Vick is stellar, but she just got engaged and she's distracted by her fiancé. And the effects coordinator has his kids on-site because his sitter was in a fender bender."

"Those are not the studio's problems. You're supposed to be finished with my place and shooting on the West Lot. Another movie is scheduled for that lot in two weeks. The studio takes a hit if they can't start production."

Ray shrugged. "Add it to the budget."

Garrett shook his head. That's exactly the attitude that led to the studio's teetering reputation. "Ray, I love you like a brother, but the days of open budgets died with my dad. You have two weeks and one million. I'm closing your set to all nonessential personnel. Get your people under control, and get it done."

Tori popped a candy-coated peanut in her mouth and surveyed the candy table. Perfect. Sticking to the colors red, black, silver and white, she'd used martini-shaped glasses large and small to create her design. Drops, gummies and foil-wrapped candies filled the dishes. White letters filled with dark chocolate-covered mints spelled out *RAY*. A black satin table cover and silver and red ribbons pulled the whole look together.

No sooner did she step back than guests converged on the treats. Oohs and aahs followed her retreat. In spite of her less than fortuitous encounter with Black, Tori counted tonight as a success. She'd received lots of compliments on the food and given their card to three prospective clients.

Reminded of Black, she moved to the entry and lingered near the living room where she had a view of the front door. Matt had found the claim ticket for the Maserati in his jacket pocket and brought it to her to pass on to the owner. She grimaced, as if she needed another run-in with Black.

As if her thoughts had conjured the man, he suddenly appeared from the crowd. And he was headed directly for her.

She summoned a smile. "Mr. Black, is there anything I can get for you?"

He lifted a dark brow at the use of his name. He glanced to the left where the food filled the table and a crowd surrounded the candy display, and then dropped to the martini glass she'd filled for herself.

"This will do." Taking the glass from her, he dumped half the contents into his hand. "Thanks."

Surprised by his sweet tooth and offended by his rudeness, she warned him, "Careful, I'm a peanut fiend, so I hope you aren't allergic."

"Nope. Did you enjoy driving my car, Ms. Randall?"

"It was the highlight of my night." She stifled any reaction to the use of her name, unable to determine if it was a good thing or bad.

"Which reminds me." With a sheepish smile she dug into her cleavage and retrieved his claim ticket. "I forgot to give you this."

He accepted the paper, looked from it to her bust. Heat flared in his gray eyes before they lifted to meet her gaze.

"Sorry," she murmured, shrugging, "no pockets."

"No need to apologize." He flicked the ticket with his thumb. "I may have to keep this as a memento of the evening."

Okay, what did that mean? Good gracious. Was he hitting on her? Wouldn't Lauren love that? As for Tori, sure he tipped the studometer, but his aloof, brooding attitude triggered one of her hot buttons, putting him off-limits even more than the fact he was a client.

Of course there was that gorgeous car. "If you need a designated driver, I'm happy to be of assistance."

"Do I appear drunk to you, Ms. Randall?" The gravel in his voice took on a gruffness.

Oops, she'd upset him again. "No, but a girl can hope."

"Very amusing."

She shrugged and was rewarded by him taking the last of her candy.

"You don't mind, do you?" he challenged her.

"Of course not." Jerk. "I can get you one of your own if you'd like."

"No, yours is good enough."

Was he trying to outdo himself in boorish behavior or was it simply his default mode? Whichever, charming he was not. Then again she didn't remember ever hearing the word attached to his name. *Hardworking, brilliant* and *brooding* were the words used to describe him. Usually as a director. Looking into his pale eyes she didn't doubt the truth of them.

As a guest, he could use a lesson in playing nice with others.

"Good night, Ms. Randall." He stepped past her toward the door.

"Drive safely, Mr. Black," she said to his back. She wouldn't want anything to happen to his beautiful car.

CHAPTER TWO

LATE MONDAY AFTERNOON Tori worked on a spreadsheet displaying the menu for a fiftieth wedding anniversary scheduled for Thursday. She was making the final notes to the grocery list when the bell over the front door sounded.

"Be right there," she called out as she took a moment to save her file. A quick glance through the glass wall of her office revealed the visitor was a man, but he had his back to her. By Arrangement rarely got drop by traffic. The nature of their business generally took them to their clients. In fact Lauren was out with a prospective client now, which left Tori to handle the man haunting their showroom.

Her toes searched under her desk for her shoes. She ended up kicking them farther back and bent to retrieve the ballerina flats. Happy she chose to wear black jeans today, which were slightly dressier than regular jeans, she walked out of her office, tugging at the hem of her olive sweater as she greeted the visitor.

"Welcome— You." She stopped short at the sight of Garrett Black. He stood tall and broad in the middle of the showroom in another ill-fitting suit. "What are you doing here?" Hearing the strident tone, she cringed. "I mean, Mr. Black, how can I help you?"

"Ms. Randall." He glanced around the converted restaurant, taking in the glass offices, the tables dressed in different styles for special occasions, the well-stocked bar. He lifted a brow at her.

"We occasionally host events here," she explained. "Or we used to." She and Lauren bought the restaurant four years ago for the kitchen because they'd outgrown her apartment kitchen for food prep. Business continued to bloom, and after six months, the front was converted to offices, storage and the current showroom.

He nodded and continued to wander. At one of the tables he picked up a fork, set it back down. His presence confused her. She and Lauren had great ideas outlined for the film festival, but the next series of meetings with Obsidian weren't scheduled until the first part of December.

"Would you like to sit?" she asked him.

"No." He faced her, shoved his hands in his coat pockets. "I've come about the toe prints."

She blinked at him. "Toe prints?"

"Yes. Upon inspection of my vehicle this morning I found toe prints on the carpet of the driver's side. I wanted to let you know I'll be forwarding the cleaning bill."

Tori listened with growing outrage. He had to be kidding. "No," she corrected, keeping her tone easy. "Remember, I was barefoot when we met, but you stopped me before I got in the car." His precious oh-so-fabulous car.

Aggravating man. How petty of him to try to get a car cleaning out of her, especially when money wasn't the issue. He was upset because she'd made him feel. Anger, arousal, humor, she'd seen flashes of each emotion in the brief conversations they'd had.

Whatever had happened to him, and it went way further back than his accident, he'd cut himself off from emotion. She imagined the accident and losing his dad only added to the pain he hid behind a brooding facade.

All too familiar with the destructive force of repressed feelings, she easily recognized the anguish simmering in his silver eyes. She felt for him, but not even his manly beauty tempted her to go there again.

Caring for an emotional recluse was equivalent to treading through a mental minefield.

"You were the only one near the car barefoot. I assume you will want to take care of this matter promptly as it would be awkward working together on the film festival with this issue unresolved."

She gritted her teeth. He was right. Having this issue hanging over By Arrangement while she worked the film festival was unacceptable. Arguing with him didn't make sense, either. Not while Black was a client.

Plus, no way did Tori want Lauren knowing about this. She would never let Tori forget the need to wear appropriate shoes if she learned Tori was being billed for footprints. Yet she still protested.

"Between the two of us I'm sure we can figure this out." Much as she disliked confrontation, Tori didn't care to be pushed around or taken advantage of, either. "Let me see the prints." She headed for the door and the parking lot beyond.

Hey, she had a right to challenge the totally bogus accusation. Innocent until proven guilty, she wanted to see the evidence, to defend her good name. The truth was she admired the beautiful machinery of the Maserati too much to mar it and she found the accusation insulting.

"You honestly believe I'd make up footprints?" The caustic question came from behind her. "For what reason? Some half-witted excuse to see you again?"

She froze with her hand on the car handle, struck by the concept. For all the derision in his words, she knew he found her attractive. Perhaps that was the answer. He was punishing them both for the chemistry between them.

And perhaps she was overthinking it. He was a jerk, reason enough for his contrary behavior.

She tried opening the door of the red Maserati Spider convertible and about pulled her shoulder from the socket when it refused to give. Locked. She turned to him, forced a smile. "Open, please."

She met stoic resistance.

What now? Then it hit her, she hadn't answered his question.

"Look, I'm not vain enough to figure you manufactured an excuse and went out of your way to pursue me. Since I didn't step barefoot into the car, I want to help you determine what it is."

"I know toe prints when I see them." But he clicked the locks, allowing her to open the door.

Bending over, she stuck her head inside. The scent of well-tended leather filled her senses. Such a sexy aroma. It made her think of smart cars, long drives and hard men. None of which were appropriate to the moment. Discounting the hardheaded male looming over her.

She ran her hand over the soft buttercream upholstery, eyed the matching carpet. Three small smudges were grouped close together. She supposed they could be toe prints, but she didn't think so.

"They look like paw prints," she said, glancing over her shoulder in time to catch him eyeing her butt. Her blood heated at the appreciation in his pale gaze. But she tamped it down as she stood and faced him, reminding herself of the complications he presented—client, tortured soul.

"Absolutely not." He denied her explanation. He stepped back and seemed to wobble a bit on the uneven asphalt. He glared at the ground before turning the look on her. "Impossible. Unless you left a window open when you parked the car."

"No. I adjusted the seat." A necessity considering, at six feet, he stood a good eight inches taller than her. "But I just pulled it into the garage. There was no need to adjust the mirrors."

"Then the only explanation is toe prints."

"Unless the marks were there before you reached the party," she offered in what she felt was a reasonable tone. "Do you inspect all areas of the car before driving it each time?"

"Of course not." He scowled, his annoyance over the discussion more than clear. "But they weren't there before."

"How do you know?"

"Because I didn't drive it barefoot. And I live alone. Not even a cat. No one else to leave toe prints or paw prints."

"Okay." She moved toward him so she could close the car door.

He took a hasty step backward, his heel landed in a small hole and his leg buckled, sending him sprawling on his butt. A grunt of pain was cut off by a string of vile curses.

It was one of those fast-forward, slow-motion moments. Tori saw the fall unfolding and reached out to grab him, but his momentum pulled his hand right through hers. She had to catch herself from falling on top of him.

"Are you okay?" Stupid question. His complexion had gone white and his jaw was clenched against the pain. She crouched next to him. "How can I help?"

"Back the hell up." He shooed her away. "Give me some room."

Respecting his wish, she stood back but watched him carefully. In high school she worked two years as a life-guard at her dad's golf club. From his paleness and the clamminess of his skin, he looked about to pass out. If that happened, she'd have to call an ambulance because there'd be no handling his deadweight.

"Garrett, are you light-headed?" She knelt next to him.

"A little," he admitted, which said a lot.

"We don't want you passing out. I would have to call an ambulance…" Mention of an ambulance got his attention.

"No hospital. I just need a moment." He supported himself on one arm, leaning sideways. The other hand clutched at his right leg, the obvious point of his pain. He tried to rise but slumped back. "My head is spinning."

"Okay, you need to sit up. And put your head in your lap." He no doubt saw spots before his eyes. She helped him into position and rubbed a hand over his back. It was supposed to be your head between your knees. She hoped this would be enough to stop the dots from merging into total darkness.

After a moment, he lifted his head. "It's better. Thanks. Sorry to snap at you."

Dark tendrils fell over his eyes. Brushing them back, she felt the dampness of his skin. It had been a close call. "Okay, let's get you on your feet."

Without asking this time, she tucked an arm under his right shoulder and lifted. He managed to get his left leg under himself, and between the two of them, he reached his feet.

He brushed off his clothes, teetering, but unwilling to ask for help.

"I'll send you a bill for the carpet cleaning." It would be a great exit line, except his right leg wouldn't hold his weight. He almost went down again when he tried.

"Enough of this." She invaded his space, cupped his face in her hands, feeling the prickle of an approaching five o'clock shadow, and met his pain-filled gaze. "Either you accept my help or I call for that ambulance. It's your choice."

Just for a moment he hooded his eyes, leaned into her touch. In the next instant, he jerked away. Squaring his shoulders, irritation stamped his features, eradicating any flash of vulnerability she may have imagined.

"No hospital." He repeated his earlier decree. "I strained

an old injury. I just need to get home and put some ice on it."

"It's your right leg. You aren't driving anywhere."

His jaw clenched as he struggled between desire and reality. "Fine." He gritted the word through his teeth. "You can drive me home."

Lucky her. As if hauling his injured rear was a highly sought after reward. She rolled her eyes, pretended her heart hadn't leaped at the notion of driving the Maserati and tucked her shoulder under his arm to help him around the car. This close he smelled of a spicy cologne touched with lavender and citrus, raw male and, oh, Lord, leather.

The sexy combination nearly knocked her on *her* tush.

Unfortunately, once they reached the passenger side, it became obvious the car was too low-slung for him to comfortably lower himself into it.

"This isn't going to work," she declared, raw with frustration.

"For once, I agree." He shifted on his good leg, and suddenly she was in his arms, her hands clutching his waist. "I need to keep my leg straight." His breath caressed her cheek, sending a shiver down her spine.

"We can use the company SUV. It's higher and has more legroom. Wait here." Relieved, she ducked out from under his arm. She blamed her near sprint inside on the need to get rid of him. She wasn't running scared.

"Liar," she muttered while snagging the keys to the fuel-friendly Ford and locking up the showroom. Wanting him gone had everything to do with running scared. And a strong sense of self-preservation. So she'd drive him home, pay to clean his blasted carpet and put him firmly from her mind.

Garrett clicked the locks on his prized Maserati, a gift to himself from the profits of his first successful film. He rued the impulse that brought him to West Hollywood and the offices of By Arrangement.

When he found the toe prints in his car this morning, he'd been annoyed.

Tori Randal's barefooted impersonation of a valet fell short of professionalism in his opinion. He'd come here today in the hopes she could redeem that impression before he put his company's reputation in her hands at the upcoming international film festival.

Of course the insolent blonde couldn't simply admit her mistake and agree to right the wrong. No, she questioned his motives and his eyesight. Whatever.

What really needed questioning was his sanity.

He should have remembered how he'd reacted to her. She glowed as only a true optimist could, lush lips too ready to smile, amber eyes sparkling, demanding everyone she came in contact with join her in the dance of life. And the long line of her ivory neck displayed by her sophisticated ponytail at the party and a serviceable braid today just made him want to take a bite.

Exactly when had he become part vampire?

During the long, lonely, pain-ridden nights since the accident came the ready answer. Better to be exhausted from physical therapy and reviewing studio business than to lay awake raked by pain and regrets.

Now he'd let the perky blonde with no sense of boundaries get to him again. And the result was a pulled muscle in his bad leg. His own damned fault, tripping over an inch-deep hole and twisting his foot. Pain had streaked up his weak leg and it gave. He'd done it before, pushing himself too far, too fast, but it still hurt like a bitch.

A white SUV pulled up next to him, and Tori hopped out and came trotting around to his side. He didn't wait for her. He opened the door, plunked his butt down and pulled his leg in.

"Oh, yeah, much better." Tori arrived in time to help lift his leg in.

"I can do it." He scowled at her, both for the interference and the cheerful optimism. "Let's just get going."

"Aye-aye." She saluted him and made the reverse trip around to the driver's seat.

He might appreciate the impertinence if he weren't in pain. And mortified. He closed his eyes, as it was he just wanted to get home.

"Here." She thrust a water bottle at him after climbing in next to him. "Do you have any pain pills with you?"

"I don't like taking pain meds." The usual protest sprang automatically to his tongue.

She gave him a schoolteacher glare, the kind that made you question your own intelligence. "That's not what I asked. If you have something with you, take it."

He glared back, not caring in the least that it screamed petulant rebellion. He may have tripped up like a little boy, but he was a grown man capable of knowing the needs of his own body.

"I can always take you to the hospital. I'm sure they'll give you something."

"Why do you care if I'm in pain?"

She looked truly confused by the question. "I care whenever anyone is in pain."

"The painkillers don't help the injury. They just mask the pain, making it possible for you to hurt yourself even more."

"The pain medicine helps you to relax. If it's a pulled muscle like you seem to think, a lessening of the tension in the muscles actually will assist in the healing process."

"They make me sleepy." It wasn't quite a whine but too close for his pride. So he dug out the pills, popped one in his mouth and chased it with a long sip of water. "You seem to know a lot about physical ailments for an event coordinator."

"I got into first aid when I was doing my lifeguard stint. Where are we going?" She'd been driving as they argued but had reached the freeway. "Do I go north or south?"

He directed her north and gave her the address, which she put in her GPS.

"I know that address. You're living at Obsidian Studios?"

"Sometimes it feels like it, but no, I'm staying at The Old Manor House."

Her head whipped his way. "How can you be living at The Old Manor House?"

He cocked a brow at her surprise. "My family does own the house."

"Of course." Eyes back on the road, she shrugged. "But I thought it was closed up."

"It was, most of it still is, but after his last divorce, my father moved back into a wing on the bottom floor." Why was he explaining anything to her? But what the heck, he preferred to be alert. Talking helped. "I'd rather go to my place on the coast in Santa Barbara, but I moved into the Hollywood mansion when I started working at the studio. It's closer, more convenient when I have to be there every day."

No need to admit driving still bothered his leg. In fact, no need to talk about himself.

"From lifeguard to event coordinator. That's quite a change. How'd that happen?"

Her luscious lips pursed. "Well, after high school we went to UCLA." Her gaze touched him for a second. "You're an alum, too."

"Yes." He agreed. "A few years before you I'm guessing."

"Four," she answered promptly.

"Very precise." Why would she know that?

A grin flashed his way. "I searched for you online. Standard research prior to putting in the bid to Obsidian Studios."

"What was your major?" He lobbed the focus back to her. Smothering a yawn, he convinced himself it was drowsiness and not disappointment he felt. Of course her research had been business related not personal.

"Communications, but I switched to business when By Arrangement came to be."

"You started your business in college?"

She laughed. "Sometimes I think we started our business in the womb. My mom is big on celebrations. Birthdays, holidays, accomplishments were all good reasons to have a party. So we grew up entertaining. When we hit the sorority at UCLA, we naturally stepped up whenever there was an event. Our reputation grew and we started doing other events around school. It started as a way to make extra money. But as people graduated, they still called us and we started doing events outside the school. Our junior year, we named our business By Arrangement, changed our majors to business and never looked back."

The love for her job rang loud in her animated chatter. The pride in her accomplishments, which she clearly shared with her sister, indicated a bond of trust and affection. From what she'd said of her mother, it sounded as if she'd had a happy childhood.

Too much cheer for him.

"I must say By Arrangement came highly recommended. Your previous clients must have missed out on the toe print experience."

In profile he watched the joy in her switch off.

He heard a sigh and then a very polite, "I'm sorry. Please send me the cleaning bill and I'll see it's paid."

Blessed silence filled the vehicle.

He turned to look unseeing out the window, feeling as if

he'd spanked a puppy. She was the one in need of a spanking. If she'd gracefully accepted the blame when he'd first arrived, he would have left immediately and been sitting down to a nice meal at Antonio's right now.

On cue his stomach rumbled.

Ignoring it, ignoring her, he closed his eyes and pretended to sleep.

Tori kept her eyes on the road. In another ten minutes she'd drop his ungrateful hide off at the curb. She couldn't wait.

Thank heavens the meds finally kicked in and he fell asleep, lifting the need for conversation. If you counted grunts and sarcasm as conversation. She got it. He'd had a bad year. But there was no reason to take it out on her.

She took the off-ramp that led to Obsidian Studios and The Old Manor House. He deserved to live alone in a spooky old place. The house got its name shortly after it was built because the house and grounds were used in an old black-and-white movie of the same name. The movie became a Gothic horror classic. It scared her spitless as a kid.

Only a few more blocks.

Then she heard it again, the rumble of his stomach. Her brow puckered as she tried to recall if he'd mentioned staff. He probably had a cook and a housekeeper, right? She had no doubt whatsoever that his father would have had a staff. But Garrett spent several months in the hospital. It was totally possible the staff had been let go. Especially as Garrett had his own home.

Dang it. Sometimes she was too nice for her own good, but she couldn't leave him at the curb both hurt and hungry.

Dark had fallen and she panned the street in front of her and then in the rearview mirror. Spotting the pink neon sign of a fast-food Chinese restaurant, she whipped a U-turn and zipped into the parking lot. Perfect.

She glanced at Garrett, who didn't move. Good. She may be willing to feed him, but she was done talking to the man. Grabbing her purse, she went inside. The savory scents of East Asia immediately enveloped the senses. The smell of garlic, ginger, onions and chicken made her mouth water.

Yes, this would do nicely for dinner. Having no idea what Garrett liked, she requested both beef and chicken items. He didn't strike her as a vegetarian. Too much the predator.

Back in the car she tucked the bags behind the passenger seat and reengaged the GPS. A few minutes later she turned into a gated drive. Of course it would have security.

Man, she'd really been anticipating the curb.

"Mr. Black," she called, hoping to rouse him. He didn't move, so she said his name again, louder. Then she shook his arm. "Garrett!"

His pale eyes opened, appearing silver in the glare of the spotlight aimed at the SUV. The light triggered when she pulled up to the security display situated just short of the ten-foot-high brick wall. Garrett blinked at her and then the house.

"We're here." His voice was thick with sleep.

"Yes. I need the code."

He rattled off a number, the gate began to open and she inched forward. A groan sounded next to her as Garrett shifted in his seat. Out of the corner of her eyes she saw him scrub his hands over his face.

Once she cleared the gate, streetlights came on showing the way to the house in the distance. She drove a quarter mile curving around to the front of the house, where the drive circled a large fountain. Six steps led up to an extensive porch. That presented a problem.

"Is there a better spot to drop you?" she asked. "An entrance without steps?"

"Yeah, pull around to the back. There are only two steps up to the back porch."

She followed his directions and stopped so her lights shined on the steps. A gray cat sprang up and darted away.

"No cat, huh?"

"I've never seen it before."

"Of course not." As if she believed that.

"And it hasn't been in my car." He opened his door and slid out. "Thanks for the ride."

"Wait." She hurried around the front of the SUV to reach his side.

"I don't need your help." He advised her, the short nap unfortunately not improving his disposition.

"Probably not." She agreed and took his arm. "You're getting it anyway. It's dark and the ground is uneven. I prefer not to take any chances."

A put-upon sigh filled the chill November evening. Once they reached the porch, he made a point of climbing them unassisted. Irritating man!

But good. She didn't need to worry about leaving him. At the bottom of the stairs she waited until he opened the door and turned on the light.

"Good night, Ms. Randall."

"Good night, Mr. Black." Good riddance, more like.

"Oh, wait." She ran to the SUV and came back with the white bag of food. Climbing to the porch she crossed to him and pushed the package into his arms. "Bon appétit. You probably shouldn't feed the cat."

CHAPTER THREE

LAUREN WALKED AROUND Tori's Mustang and slid into the passenger seat as her sister made her way to the back door of The Old Manor House. She heard Tori's knock just before she closed the door.

Lauren wasn't sure she bought Tori's explanation that Black had been driving by and decided to stop by their showroom to introduce himself. But there had to be some truth to the part where he hurt his leg and couldn't drive or he never would have left his Maserati.

The light over the back door came on and Garrett Black opened the door. He stepped outside wearing only a pair of low hanging gray sweatpants and nothing more. Oh, my. She found his muscular physique impressive even as far away as the vehicle where she sat. The two exchanged words and for a moment she envied Tori her closer view.

But then she felt the warmth growing in her chest. Her eyes went wide as the feeling grew. It dimmed as Tori moved away from Black, stomped down the steps and got back in Garret's car. Across the way a garage door opened. Tori drove the Maserati inside.

She reappeared, returned to the back porch and dropped the keys into Black's outstretched hand with more force than necessary. The closer Tori drew to Black, the stronger the warmth bloomed in Lauren's chest. Distracted by the discovery, she jumped when Tori suddenly opened the driver's door and slid inside.

"Ungrateful beast." Tori slammed the Mustang in Reverse.

"He wasn't happy to have his car returned?"

"Not in the least." Gravel sprayed as she headed for the gate. "Nobody drives his car but him."

"You drove it the other night." Lauren pointed out.

"That's what I said. It appears valets are an exception."

She laughed at Tori's outrage and decided to test her. "You like him."

"Are you insane?" Tori exclaimed, sending Lauren a sideways glare. "The man has the manners of a mule."

"And the body of a stud."

Her twin remained silent until they cleared the gate and turned toward the freeway.

"Come on, Tori. You're not blind."

She rolled her eyes, but Lauren saw the corner of her sister's mouth twitch.

"OMG, he's hot." Tori fanned herself. "He had to repeat himself because I was staring. It was mortifying."

Oh, yeah. There was no doubt in Lauren's mind. Tori had met her match.

"I'm ready to take out a contract on Garrett Black," Jenna Vick announced and took a sip of her margarita. "Mark has been banned from the set. Work has become such a drudge."

Thinking of her encounters with Black, of his unsmiling facade and his penchant for being a bit of a jerk, Tori wasn't totally shocked by the redhead's reaction to the man. What a shame such a gorgeous car belonged to such a dysfunctional individual.

"Count me in." Cindy Tate tucked a wisp of blond hair behind her ear before tapping her glass to Jenna's. "My

TERESA CARPENTER   37

mother came to town to see me work. She'd really been looking forward to being on the set. But the guards refused to let her join me. I asked for a few days off to spend with her and was told no because the film is behind schedule."

"I'll pitch in," Olivia Fox chimed, not moving an inch as she basked, tanned and toned, in the sunshine, her jet-black hair flowing over her bright yellow bikini.

"Did you have someone banned, too?" Jenna asked. The three actresses were rising stars working together on a futuristic action film, kind of a *Charlie's Angels* in space.

"No." Olivia adjusted her sunglasses, then resumed her boneless position. "But the set has become a morgue. Everyone is so serious and intent on their job, no one laughs anymore."

Remembering the threat of a cleaning bill for nonexistent toe prints, Tori controlled the urge to offer her own funds. Obviously the man was making friends wherever he went.

"Why do you blame Black?" Tori asked as she met Lauren's gaze across the deck, where they were all gathered at Jenna's Venice Beach home. They'd taken care of the plans for Jenna's engagement party, and were now relaxing poolside, enjoying the ocean view.

By Arrangement would be working with Black on several events when the Hollywood Hills Film Festival started in a month. Actually make that working *for* Black, which suited Tori much better. It meant she'd be less likely to run into the man.

Either way Tori knew Lauren had her ears perked, she inhaled information and used it like a weapon.

"Because it's Black's decree." Cindy rolled her eyes and touched her tongue to the salt rimming her glass. "Visitors have been limited on all sets. But if a film is over budget or over schedule, he closes the set down altogether."

"Lucky me," Jenna groused. "I'm going from one Obsidian production to another, so I get no break." She sank onto a lounger next to Olivia. "It was really nice having Mark on the set. Now I hardly get to see him." Gesturing to Tori and Lauren, she implored them to understand. "You two introduced us. You must know how much I miss him."

"Not to mention it's going to be much harder planning the wedding now," Cindy pointed out helpfully. "Tori and Lauren are great." She flashed a grin at them. "They introduced me to my hubby, too, and they gave me a spectacular wedding. Still they did need occasional input."

Lauren choked on a sip of iced tea. Probably remembering the fit Cindy threw when they went off-line for a Saturday wedding three months before her event. She wanted to tell them about a wine she tasted at a local winery she just had to have at her reception. When Lauren checked her voice mail, they had over fifty messages and had been fired. Twice. All this was after they'd advised her they had a wedding and would be unavailable. Never had Tori been happier that Lauren was the voice of By Arrangement.

Tori didn't do confrontation.

Lauren thrived on it, in a calm, controlled manner, of course.

She let Cindy vent for a couple of minutes, made noises of sympathy for her distress, showed regret for losing the contract and then hit her with the fact By Arrangement would be billing her for the work already done. Lauren wrapped it up in a pretty little bow, reminding Cindy they had told her they would be unavailable and of the clause in the contract stating on the day of a wedding By Arrangement gave the bride and her event our exclusive attention. It was a courtesy we extended to our brides and it wasn't something we were willing to compromise on. The clincher was our disappointment as we introduced Cindy to her fiancé.

Cindy apologized for her snit, which wasn't her first or her last, and By Arrangement went on to give her a "spectacular" wedding.

"We do need input," Lauren agreed, calm as always. "But you needn't worry. It's our job to make the whole process easy for you."

"But I'm getting married in March," Jenna said, pouting, "I planned to take a couple of weeks for a honeymoon, but it's in the middle of my next film. Now I'll be lucky to get a few days off."

Tori sympathized with her friend and client. She genuinely liked these women, but seriously, Jenna did sign a contract. It was a tad unrealistic to expect an entire production to halt filming so she could honeymoon. Not that Tori could voice her opinion to these three. They weren't used to being thwarted. They were in demand, which pretty much meant they got whatever they asked for. Tori supposed they could be forgiven for being a bit full of themselves.

"Obviously Garrett Black has no life or he'd understand our plight." Cindy sighed.

"From what I hear, Black is spending all his time in his office. Probably reviewing all the production contracts so he can collect on deadline penalties." Jenna scowled into her drink, absently running a finger around the rim of her glass, knocking off all the salt. "My last three projects ran over. Doesn't he realize delays are the nature of this business?"

"Were all the films Obsidian productions?" Lauren asked.

Jenna shook her head, ginger curls flowing over her bare shoulders. "Just this one, but we used Obsidian Studio's lots for the other two. And we were delayed because the lots weren't available when we were supposed to shoot. Which proves my point."

"Black is new to the job," Tori pointed out, though she had no idea why she felt compelled to defend him. "Maybe he's just trying to fix a problem he sees."

"Do not defend the man." Cindy shook a finger at Tori. "He's a coldhearted bastard."

Yeah, no argument there.

"What he needs is a woman." Olivia sat forward and wrapped her arms around her knees. "He's all work and no play. And he wants the rest of the world to be the same. If he had a woman in his life, he'd have less time to mess with ours."

"Yes." Jenna hopped up and began to pace excitedly. "A woman would distract him, soften him. He'd be more understanding of other people's relationships. He definitely needs a woman."

Uh-oh. Tori saw where this headed. She glanced at Lauren and knew her twin had come to the same conclusion. But the ball was rolling. There was no stopping it now.

"It's the perfect solution," Cindy agreed, blue eyes alight as she shifted her gaze between Lauren and Tori. "And we know the perfect pair to find her for him."

"Oh, no, he did not." A few days later, Tori clicked on an email to open it because the preview couldn't be right. Garrett Black hadn't actually sent her a bill for the cleaning of his car's carpet. But, oh yeah, he had. The attachment confirmed it: two hundred dollars for an interior cleaning.

TO: trandall@byarrangement.com
FROM: garrett.black@obsidianstudios.com
SUBJECT: Cleaning bill

Ms. Randall, please forgive my delay in providing the bill for the carpet cleaning of my Maserati. I appreciate your willingness to take responsibility for your actions. It gives me hope By Arrangement will conduct themselves in a professional manner while representing Obsidian Studios at the upcoming film festival. You may send a check to me care of the studio.

Why was she even surprised? If she looked up his birth certificate, she'd see the *A* in Garrett A. Black stood for *arrogant*. He had some nerve talking about professionalism while blaming her for toe prints that were clearly paw prints.

Obviously her gesture in returning his car to him had counted for nothing. So okay, her motive had been purely selfish. She wanted the car gone so she didn't have to deal with him again.

By taking the car to him, she controlled the where, when and how long.

What she hadn't planned on was finding him half-naked. The man was seriously built, broad shoulders, muscular arms and oh, those abs. He'd been ill, okay laid up with a broken leg. He had no right to look so good. Flustered, she'd embarrassed herself by staring.

He'd thanked her at the same time he made his annoyance clear; declaring he never left the car out at night. It wasn't enough she went out of her way to return his car; he had to guilt her into moving the car into the garage for him.

She managed to keep her cool by remembering they would be working together very soon. Something she kept in mind as she replied to his email.

TO: garrett.black@obsidianstudios.com
FROM: trandall@byarrangement.com
SUBJECT: Re: Cleaning bill

Mr. Black, it distresses me to think of your lovely vehicle being marred in any way. Payment will be forwarded promptly.
PS: How is the cat?

"I knew this matchmaking thing was going to bite us in the butt someday," Lauren announced in the car on the way to an impromptu meeting with Obsidian Studios.

"Yes," Tori agreed. "But I always thought it would be a failed relationship that caused the problem. I mean, really, we have a 100 percent success rate. You'd think one of the couples would experience troubles."

"True. Even Kate and Brad from high school are still going strong. I was talking to Mom the other day and she mentioned they're expecting their third child."

"That's so cool." She pleated her skirt and thought about her gift. "How does it feel for you?" She glanced at Lauren. "When you know two people belong together?"

For a full heartbeat, her twin met her gaze before turning back to the road. "It's a warm glow, like a surge of happiness, when I see them together."

"Me, too." Tori nodded. "It's a total sense of rightness. But I have to see them together. I never get a sense someone would be good with anyone else."

"No, me, neither," Lauren confirmed. "And we're stronger when we're together."

"I've noticed that, too. And only with people who are open."

"What do you mean?" Lauren frowned at her.

"Some people are more open than others." Tori tried to explain what she'd always felt but never expressed. "Sometimes I can actually pick up on moods if they're strong enough—happiness, sadness, fear, anger, guilt."

"Sorry to tell you this, sis, but those emotions are pretty easy to read."

"Ha-ha." Her sister completely missed the chiding glance Tori sent her. "I mean from across the room. People I don't even know. Do you ever get that?"

Lauren lifted the shoulder closest to Tori and let it drop. "Yeah, I guess. If I concentrate. I choose not to concentrate."

"I know, me, too." It was uncomfortable picking up on other people's emotions. Made her feel intrusive. "But if they're close I get blips of emotion. I think that's what we're cluing into when we feel the connection."

"Okay, that makes sense. Why all the psychoanalysis?" A touch of irritation crept into Lauren's voice.

"Because Black is as closed up as a teenage girl's locked diary. Standing or sitting right next to him, I got nothing."

"Really?" Lauren sounded surprised, drawing Tori's gaze to her profile. "You get no feeling from him at all?"

"No. Why? Did you?" Tori turned as much as the seat belt would allow. "You didn't mention you saw Black at the party."

"There was no reason to since you'd already advised me it was best not to introduce ourselves. But I saw you chatting with him before he left."

"Did you see him steal my candy?" Jerk. Lauren gave her "the look," the one that said "focus." "Okay, not relevant. Still, it wasn't nice."

"Tori."

"Right. So did you get a read on him with anyone? It would really help if you did, because the starlet trio is counting on us."

Quiet filled the car for a moment and then she muttered, "I'm not sure."

Tori started to ask what she meant but they'd reached the studio. Lauren turned into the drive and up to the guard station. She gave their names and was directed to a building two down and one over, top floor.

Once they were in the elevator, Tori demanded her sister explain her comment.

"I just meant we told Jenna, Cindy and Olivia we'd try to find someone for Black. We didn't make any promises. They don't know how it works for us."

"No, but they're going to be looking for results. And there's no dodging them, either. We're working with them on the engagement party, the bridal shower and the wedding. We need to keep them happy or life will be miserable."

"I hear you. But we aren't responsible if we don't have access to the man. They think we will because we're handling the events for Obsidian at the film festival, but the likelihood of us actually interacting with Black is very slim."

Tori liked the way her sister thought. It was the perfect out. For the matchmaking and for her. She wasn't looking forward to encountering Garrett Black again. He bothered her in a curious way. It was the brooding. She never did well with brooding.

Her chest constricted as memories rose up. The slow pulling back, the moodiness, that tragic final call.

Shane. She hadn't purposely tried to tune into anyone since she tried to read him at the height of his withdrawal. The pain and anger had overwhelmed her to the point she never tried again. And she really had no interest in putting any feelers out to Garrett Black. She'd learned her lesson there.

Thankfully the elevator opened into a reception area. From sheer force of will, she pushed the past back where it belonged and followed Lauren to a wide glass desk. Lauren gave the thirty-something blonde manning the desk their names.

"Welcome." The woman immediately bounced to her feet. "Mr. Black is expecting you." The woman came around the desk to lead them toward an inner door.

Behind her back Lauren mouthed, "Black?"

Tori shrugged, no happier than her sister at the prospect of a meeting with Black. Mystified, Tori followed Lauren toward the inner sanctum. What was this all about? They received a call at By Arrangement yesterday requesting this meeting regarding the film festival. There had been no mention of Black's involvement.

She stutter-stepped, dread filling her. Had he called them here to fire By Arrangement? Had she not been fast enough, humble enough in her acquiescence to his demand for payment? She suddenly regretted the jab about the cat.

If it were just her, she'd suck it up, take the loss and move on. But there was Lauren. The contract with Obsidian Studios was the biggest and most prestigious By Arrangement had earned. It was the first true step on the road to their goal of staging the ultimate Hollywood party, the Governors Ball after the Academy Awards.

Plus they'd already put a lot of time and effort into the plans for the film festival. She hated confrontation, but for Lauren she would fight.

She wouldn't let Black blow them off over a set of toe prints.

"Ms. Randall, Tori." Garrett stood up as she entered the room behind Lauren. Gone were the ill-fitting suits. He looked imposing in an impeccable black suit custom-made to fit the broad stretch of his shoulders. He waved them to a conversation area near windows overlooking the back lots. "Please have a seat. I'm expecting Kira, who you've been working with, but I've also asked the head of the PR department to join us."

"I don't understand, Mr. Black." Lauren gracefully sank into the corner of a black leather couch. "Do you have a problem with the plans we sent over? We received notice they'd been approved."

Tori felt the weight of Garrett's pale gaze as she sat down. She released the button on her navy blazer and crossed one bare leg over the other, meeting him stare for stare.

"I've seen the plans," he said, turning his attention to Lauren. "They are quite ambitious, but I want Obsidian to make an impression at the film festival, so yes, I approve.

I've asked you here because I want to add an event to those already contracted."

Another event? Tori was already anticipating the end of the film festival and putting Black behind them and he wanted to add another event?

Tori met Lauren's gaze. As he'd stated, their schedule was already ambitious. Lauren gave a slight nod. Tori sighed. What the heck, go big or go home. It was a lesson they learned at their father's knee.

"Of course," Lauren stated with confidence. "What did you want to add?"

"A ninetieth anniversary celebration."

CHAPTER FOUR

"Wow." Tori fought to control her expression. "How many people were you thinking of for this event?"

"I don't know." He shrugged. "Maybe three hundred."

She met Lauren's gaze, saw the figures were already running through her head. Really? A small, intimate affair would be one thing, but an anniversary party? That sounded huge.

Time for a dose of reality.

"It's going to be really difficult to find a venue for a party that size. Between the film festival and the holidays everything is booked up."

A knock sounded and the door swung open. A plump redhead with amazing skin and a slender African-American woman with a mass of braids drawn up in a high ponytail entered the room. Garrett stood and introduced the public relations manager, Irene Allan, and Kira respectively, and then caught them up on the details discussed.

"I don't understand, sir." Kira sat braced on the edge of her seat as if ready to hop into action or flee at a moment's notice. "We have a yearlong campaign planned for the ninetieth anniversary ready to launch in January."

"Yes, and the film festival gets a lot of national coverage. The anniversary is actually in December. I want to take advantage of the celebrities and exposure already provided by the event." He focused his silver eyes on Tori. "Surely something is available."

"Possibly," She tried for optimism. "If you're willing to go outside of Hollywood Hills—"

"No." Black gave an emphatic shake of his head. "It has to be in Hollywood Hills. I want there to be no doubt the party is part of the film festival. And we have to find a place quickly. I talked to the head of the film festival. We have a week to provide the venue information for it to be included in the program."

"Garrett." Pale eyes narrowed. She cleared her throat. "Ah, Mr. Black, nothing is available in Hollywood Hills. I received two calls this week asking if our plans were finalized because they were looking to take over our space."

"I got the same calls," Kira confirmed.

"Mr. Black," Lauren began in her conciliatory tone, "considering our time constraints, perhaps we can compromise. There are some very nice hotels in Beverly Hills within ten miles—"

"The Old Manor House," Tori blurted.

"—of the film festival." Lauren turned an inquiring glance Tori's way. "Excuse me?"

"Sorry." She sent her sister an apologetic smile. "I just thought of the perfect place. The Old Manor House."

"Absolutely not." Black cut her off. "That's not an option."

"Thanksgiving is this week, which means we really only have four days. The Old Manor House is perfect," she repeated. "It's in Hollywood Hills. It's iconic Obsidian Studios. And people will flock to the event to see it."

"I said no. The place is in no shape for a party."

"We have three weeks. If we start now—"

"You have my answer." He stood and buttoned his jacket. "Find me a venue close to the film festival."

* * *

"Mom and Dad will be here in an hour." Lauren propped a shoulder against the door of Tori's office. "We should head home. Any luck with the venue?"

"Two. One that exceeds our approved budget and one that's below our usual standards. I have a third but it's outside the perimeter Black set. The man is beyond stubborn."

"Look, I agree The Old Manor House is no-brainer the best option for the party. But Black is living in the house now and according to you his father was living there at the time he died. I can understand why he might not want to have a party there."

"I suppose." Okay, Tori grudgingly acknowledged she hadn't considered the father angle. Hard to when Garrett appeared so closed off emotionally. "That doesn't change the fact he's set an impossible task."

"He's the client." Lauren crossed her arms over her chest. "Have you gone over the pros and cons of the venues with Kira?"

"Yes. She's as frustrated as I am. This has been a colossal waste of time."

"Tell me about it. Forget the need to know for the program, we need to know what we'll be working with."

"You're right." Tori turned to her computer, picked up the email she sent to Kira with the venue links, made a couple of changes and hit Send. "It's in his hands now."

Lauren rolled her eyes. "Tell me you didn't do something rash."

"Just gave our client his options. Besides tomorrow is Thanksgiving. Time was up." She closed down her computer and felt around for her shoes. She refused to think of Garrett Black and his impossible demands any longer. "Let's go home. I'm anxious to see Mom and Dad. I'm really looking forward to a family Thanksgiving. I thought we were going to miss it this year."

"Me, too." Lauren linked her arm through Tori's and drew her over to Lauren's office, where she grabbed her purse from the corner of her desk before they headed for the door. "Are you sure you're up to cooking? I can still call in a favor and put in an order for turkey and all the trimmings, but tomorrow it will be too late."

"No." Tori locked up. "I miss cooking. Plus I did a bunch of prep work here today. It's already packed in the car. And I plan to put you to work to give Mom a break." She laughed as Lauren cringed. "Relax, I'm keeping it simple."

"Good. Because I plan to be on the couch watching football with Dad and Nick."

Tori's turn to send her eyes rolling. Her thing with Dad was cars, Lauren's was football. "You can peel potatoes while sitting on the couch."

"Oh. You're too kind."

"Remember that when it comes to cleanup."

"Mom put that knife down." Tori took a paring knife from her mother on the way to removing the turkey from the oven. "You're a guest this year. Oh, this smells great." She set the roasting pan on a wooden cutting board on the granite island.

"I want to help," Liz Randall protested. "I'm family, not a guest. What a beautiful bird." Mom squeezed Tori's shoulders.

"We need to let this rest. You always cook." Tori turned and gave Mom a real hug. The kitchen light bounced off the golden highlights in her new short bob. Tori thought her mother was beautiful. Young and vital, she took good care of herself and Dad. "I want you to enjoy yourself today."

"Hug fest!" Lauren suddenly threw her arms around them and the love multiplied by three. "This is better than an extra point."

"Wow, praise indeed." Mom stepped back and tweaked

both her and Lauren's hair. "My babies all grown up. So tell me, any new men in your lives?"

"Mom!" she and Lauren chorused.

"Well I'd like to hold some babies." Mom was unapologetic as she reclaimed the knife Tori had taken from her. She went to work on the chives for the mashed potatoes. "So spill."

"Tori has a nemesis," Lauren volunteered.

"Right, throw me under the bus." Tori wondered briefly how Garrett would spend the day. Did he have extended family or was he now alone in the world?

"I have nothing to share." Lauren plucked a carrot from the veggie tray. "And don't try to pretend you're not obsessed with Black."

"Now this sounds promising." Mom stole the carrot from Lauren. "You'll spoil your appetite." She pointed the carrot at Tori before popping it in her mouth. "I want all the details."

"Forget it." Tori chopped her hand through the air. "I refuse to let that man ruin my Thanksgiving."

"Spoilsport," Lauren teased and then groaned when her phone rang. "It's Ray Donovan."

"Don't answer." The words flew from Tori's mouth. "It's Thanksgiving. He has no right to expect us to be working."

"Ray Donovan the director?" Mom demanded. "Of course you have to answer. He's an important man."

"He's a client."

"You called him an arrogant jerk." Not that he'd ever been less than charming to Tori, but this was their only day off.

"I know." Lauren bit her lip, clearly torn. "I have to take this. Hello." She carried the phone out the back door, her greeting cut off as it closed.

"Ray Donovan is a jerk?" Mom's disappointment made Tori feel guilty.

"Not really. But he and Lauren have had a couple of altercations."

"I didn't think I'd have to worry about holidays being interrupted by emergencies when I married a dentist, but it's happened a few times. And, of course, it happens to your brother, the doctor, all the time." Mom stirred the gravy. "But never in a million years would I have guessed you girls got emergency calls."

"We're in the service industry." A taste of the sweet potatoes confirmed they were ready. "You'd be surprised at what people believe our availability should be. And the more VIP they get, the worse they are."

"So your success is your own downfall?" As usual Mom's perception cut to the heart of the matter.

"Yep." Tori glanced at Lauren's back, wondering why she'd even had her phone on. "But we love the work, so mostly it's okay. What's up?" she asked as Lauren stepped back inside.

"He has an unexpected guest for the holiday. He was hoping we could pull off a miracle for him."

"At three o'clock on the holiday? That would be a miracle. They'd be better off going out to dinner."

"I suggested that or that he try ordering in."

"Ha." Tori scoffed. "Pizza maybe."

"Well…"

Tori got a bad feeling. Very carefully she set the stirring spoon on a trivet. "Lauren, what did you do?"

"Don't worry. I told him our family was in town and we were about to sit down to our own meal."

Knowing her sister too well to relax, Tori propped her hands on her hips. "And?"

Lauren sighed. "And he invited us all to his place."

"Eee!" Mom slapped a hand over her mouth. "Sorry."

Tori narrowed her eyes at Lauren.

"What's up?" Dad and Nick loomed large on the family room side of the island, drawn by Mom's scream.

"Ray Donovan has invited us to his house for Thanksgiving dinner." Mom's excitement showed in the flap of her hands.

"The director of *Bots and Cops* Ray Donovan?" Dad demanded. "You know Donovan?

"Good flick." Nick chomped a celery stick.

"He's a client," Lauren informed them and slid closer to Mom, dodging Tori's glare.

"He wants our turkey," she stated baldly. "Not us."

"Yes." At least Lauren made no attempt to sugarcoat the truth. "But he said he and his friend would appreciate the company. I guess the friend has had a tough year."

"I think we should go," Nick said.

"Seriously?" Tori looked at the meal ready to be plated. What was Nick thinking?

"It's a day of thanks and of giving. We're very lucky in what we have." Nick clapped Dad on the shoulder as he included the rest of them in a sweeping glance. "We can show our thanks by sharing with those less fortunate than us."

"You know we'd be eating in a Malibu mansion?" Tori clarified.

"Money is not what's important today." Mom added her support. She kissed Tori's cheek. "I'll help you pack this up."

"Okay." She sighed. "But it's all going to have to be reheated. I don't want to hear a single word about dry turkey."

An hour later Nick pulled to a stop behind a red Maserati in Donovan's driveway.

Dad whistled from his seat in the front. "Now there's a sweet ride."

Tori exchanged looks with Lauren.

"You owe me so big for this," she warned her sister.

"What is it?" Mom gazed back and forth between them.

"Who," Lauren corrected. "Her nemesis."

Garrett sipped a beer and pretended interest in the football game Ray had on the big screen TV. His buddy demanded Garrett come over when he heard Garrett intended to spend the holiday alone.

It sounded like a good idea at the time, but he should have stayed at the manor. Or gone home to Santa Barbara, now that the film had wrapped up. He was poor company. The accident that killed his father happened a year ago.

Lonely, between wives, good old dad had shown up at Garrett's asking if he wanted to get a meal together. They usually spoke once or twice a year, but it had been a while so he agreed. They talked about a whole lot of nothing. And at the end of the night his dad was dead.

Who knew he'd actually care.

The doorbell sounded. Ray hopped up.

"More company?"

"Dinner." Ray rubbed his hands together.

"Pizza?" Garrett guessed. The meal of champions suited him fine. He wasn't real hungry. Much better than the lobster Thermidor his father had ordered for them at his club last year.

"We can do better than that." Ray headed for the door. "I invited the Randall twins and their family to join us."

The beer bottle froze halfway to Garrett's mouth and he stared unseeing at the eighty yard runback on the screen. Tori Randall was here? Definitely should have stayed home.

"Come on." Ray slapped him on the back. "You can help bring in the turkey."

Oh, joy. Garrett finished the beer he'd been nursing. Suddenly a bit of a buzz seemed like a good idea.

He arrived outside to find everyone surrounding his car and introductions being made. There were worse ways to spend a few minutes, so he popped the hood. Talk of cars and motors relaxed him some. Having a common interest eased the awkwardness of strangers thrown together.

Ray wandered off with Lauren and Mrs. Randall. The Randall men were affable and intelligent, and best of all, wanted nothing more from him than to talk cars. They had no idea to pitch, no complaint to lodge. Garrett relaxed even more.

Until he glanced up to see Tori petting the slick red paint. He felt every stroke as if she touched flesh instead of metal. She'd been present but quiet, observing rather than participating, allowing him to ignore her.

No more. His body stirred. He needed a distraction now.

"So I heard you brought turkey," he said when she lifted her gaze to his.

"Yes." She shifted her weight from one foot to the other and his eyes followed the sway of her hips in skintight jeans. Her deep rust top, lower in the back than the front, brought out the honey-brown of her eyes. "We brought the full deal."

"I can't wait. I'm starved." Nick clapped a hand down on Garrett's shoulder. "Don't get me wrong. The women in my family can cook. But Tori's idea of snacks is a few veggie sticks. A man needs substance on Thanksgiving."

"You're a doctor." Tori's hands landed on her hips, highlighting the sweet curves of her body. "You should be touting the value of vegetables as a snack. I swear, it's a wonder you aren't three hundred pounds."

"Hey, it takes a lot of calories to put in ten-hour days."

"Time on the golf course doesn't count."

"Ha-ha. At least I exercise."

Nick led the way to the back of the SUV and opened the hatch door. Heavenly scents hit Garrett's nostrils. That quickly, his appetite flared and he was as hungry as Nick professed to be.

"I exercise."

"Right, you shake your butt to music twice a week."

"Zumba is not for the weak. We'll put it on later and see who outlasts whom."

Obviously a well-worn argument between the siblings. Garrett hoped they moved off topic soon. Images of Tori wiggling her behind until sweat glistened on her skin felt like punches to his gut. And did nothing to cool down his libido.

"Children, no arguing in front of company."

Her father's playful chiding brought a rosy glow to Tori's cheeks.

Garrett sighed and reached for a box, resolving to ignore the woman at all costs. What had Ray been thinking to invite the Randall family to dinner? Of course Garrett knew. His well-intentioned friend meant to take Garrett's mind off memories of last year.

Hefting his box, he followed Tori's tight backside up the front steps. Damned if Ray hadn't succeeded.

Heating up the meal barely took any time at all. Unfortunately. At least she was safe in the kitchen. Tori didn't have to fear where she looked in case she happened to link gazes with the head of Obsidian Studios.

Safe? Fear? Strange words.

Why did Garrett disconcert her so much? She wasn't afraid of him. She'd experienced his bark and lived through it. She didn't fear him physically. No, she wasn't afraid of his bite. But the thought of his touch? That disturbed her.

Because she wanted it too much.

Sweet sunflowers but she wanted his hands on her. He felt it, too. He liked to pretend he didn't. Right. As if the chemistry between them didn't sizzle like an electrical current.

But Garrett had issues. She saw them clearly in his eyes—when he allowed anything to show. More often he kept his feelings locked carefully away. That, too, was a clue to his lack of emotional availability.

Tori didn't do issues.

Sure, everyone carried baggage. But some felt things more deeply than others. Some brooded, which allowed the pain to continually rise to the surface no matter how hard they tried to bury it. The problem was if they never dealt with the issue, if they never got to the other side of anger or denial, they didn't heal, and they became a powder keg of emotion.

She knew from personal experience if he blew when he was in a bad place, the result could be fatal.

She didn't want to go there again.

So she, too, avoided the sizzle.

"Your dad likes your young man." Mom strolled in from setting the table.

The plate of asparagus landed on the counter with more force than Tori intended, causing a clatter and one of the spears to roll off. She scooped it up and threw it away.

"What are you talking about, Mom?" She wiped her hands down the front of her black apron.

"Don't play dumb, dear. Garrett Black. You're smitten."

"No, I'm not." Refusing to give her mother any encouragement, Tori moved the asparagus to a tray along with the potatoes and gravy. They'd be eating family style at the dining room table.

"There's something there." Mom grabbed the butter and corn pudding and followed Tori through to the dining room. "I've seen the way you look at each other."

"Shh. He'll hear you." But a peek at the group in front of the TV showed Garrett occupied in the game. Obviously sides had been chosen and the lead depended on the field goal about to be kicked.

She returned to the kitchen for the turkey. Thrusting the broccoli salad into her mother's hands, she declared, "He's a client, Mom. I don't get personally involved with clients."

"No?" Mom lifted the salad bowl and arched a finely plucked brow.

"Today is an exception," she insisted. "And Lauren's fault."

"True, but I'm not sorry we came. Ray Donovan is charming. Your father and Nick are having a great time and I'll have something to tell all my friends when we return to Palm Springs." She set the dish down to hug Tori. "And I'm glad you're getting a chance to spend time with Garrett. You're an event coordinator, kiddo, not a doctor. There's no reason once the film festival is over that you can't see where the attraction between the two of you leads."

"Mom." Love and exasperation filled the word.

"Tori." Stubbornness and affection came back at her.

"It smells delicious in here." A male voice broke into the standoff. "Can I help with anything?"

"Garrett." Surprise added a bit of a squeak to his name. Lord, had he heard her conversation with Mom? His stoic expression gave nothing away. She cleared her throat. "Dinner is ready."

"You're just in time to carry in the turkey." Mom handed Tori the broccoli salad and, hooking her arm through Garrett's, led him to the platter holding the holiday bird. "It's quite heavy."

"Sure," Garrett said.

"Excellent." Mom released him and moved away. "Tori will help you. I'll go rally the troops."

Tori glared at her mother's disappearing back. Subtle, much?

"This looks wonderful." Garrett leaned over the turkey and took a big whiff before lifting his gaze to Tori. "It's been a long time since I actually had a traditional Thanksgiving meal."

Something in his tone made her think there was more to his statement than the surface meaning.

"Many families have traditions besides turkey." Tori sought to ease any awkwardness. "What does your family do?"

"Nothing."

She laughed. "Kind of like us, huh?" She waved in the direction of the living room. "Football and turkey is it for us. But it's all about getting together, isn't it?"

"When I said 'nothing,' I meant nothing. It was only my dad and me. Last year was the first time we'd gotten together in years. It was the last time I saw him. I'll take this through." He picked up the heavy platter and carried it to the adjoining dining room.

Oh, God. No wonder Ray called them. Tori rubbed at a pain over her left eye, extracted her foot from her mouth and followed Garrett.

Surprisingly, she thoroughly enjoyed dinner. The TV was muted at Mom's insistence, which allowed for discussion. Dad said grace and then the food began to flow around the table. As host, Ray cut the turkey. Garrett ribbed him some, but it was all in fun.

Nick asked Ray about his last megahit and he entertained them with stories from the set of that movie and several others. He drew Garrett into the conversation and he lit up as he recalled some outrageous incidences from his films. For the first time she saw his passion for his work.

Thank goodness. After his revelation in the kitchen, she'd worried he might brood through the meal. She actually caught herself staring when he laughed. Had she never heard him laugh before? Now she thought about it, no. He was always so somber.

Dad and Nick threw in a few humorous stories from the dentist office and hospital. She shared a glance with Lauren, and they silently agreed not to join the trend. Yeah they had funny and outrageous stories about events they'd handled. Still, it wouldn't be smart to share with clients at the table.

"I made pumpkin pie for dessert," Mom announced. A round of groans flowed around the table followed by a flood of compliments aimed at Tori for the meal just consumed.

"Thanks," she responded, pleased by the appreciation. "I seriously want some pie, Mom, but I have to wait for a while."

The others wholeheartedly agreed. Ray and Garrett both showed interest when Lauren mentioned the annual poker game.

"Okay." Nick rubbed his hands together. "Let's get the table cleared and get started."

"Don't worry about the dishes. My staff will clean up tomorrow." Ray picked up his plate and headed for the kitchen. "I have a game table upstairs in the loft. I'll go get it set up."

"I'll help." Lauren dropped off her plate and joined Ray.

A warm feeling swelled behind Tori's heart, bringing her to a dead stop as the two of them walked by. Hmm. There was definitely more than antagonism between the two of them. She'd have to tag Lauren for more information tomorrow.

She continued to the sink, began to run hot water.

A large hand reached past her and turned it off. "Ray said his staff would take care of the cleanup."

Garrett. Who knew he spent so much time in the kitchen?

"Yes, but I have to clean my containers." Forget leftovers, two extra male appetites took care of those. "Plus I should rinse the dishes. It'll only take a few minutes."

"I can't let you do that." He took the sponge from her hand. "You cooked. You shouldn't have to do dishes, too."

"Well, if you insist." She stepped aside and waved him into place. "I'll stack the dishwasher."

Dark brows lifted, but he accepted the challenge by rolling up his sleeves and stepping up to the sink. He brandished the rinse wand like a pro.

"Garrett, how sweet of you to help." Mom came in with the last of the serving dishes. "I'll scrape and we'll have these done in no time."

"Mom, you don't have to help." Tori tried to protest, but her mother waved her off much as Tori had tried to wave off Garrett. Once Mom finished her self-imposed chore, she went in search of dirty dishes in the living room, brought her collection into them and bustled off again.

"She's a bit of a dynamo, isn't she?" Garrett muttered. "I can see where you girls get your energy."

Girls? "You say that like it's a bad thing."

"No, but it can be unnerving." He handed her the last container, leaned back against the counter and reached for a dishrag to dry his hands. "It's also easy to see where you get your looks. Your father is a lucky man."

Oh. She smiled slightly. So he did find her attractive. Not that it mattered. Too many strikes against them. She dried the last of her containers and tucked it in a box. Looking down she realized she still wore her apron. With a grimace she pulled it off and tucked it in the box, too. No wonder he thought she looked like her mother.

"Thanks for the help. I'm going to run this stuff out to the car." She lifted one of the two boxes she'd brought the food in and set it on the rolling cooler.

"Let me." He set the other box on top and began rolling. He took it out the back door and they walked down the drive.

Tori shivered. Salt and smoke from a fireplace scented

the air. Dark hid the ocean view. And a low marine layer obscured the stars.

"It looks like we'll have fog tonight. We probably shouldn't stay too late."

"Yeah, I feel the damp in my leg."

Oh, man, she couldn't catch a break. He'd actually been decent today, participating in the conversation, helping with the chores. And she kept reminding him of all he'd lost. She watched while he packed the boxes and cooler in the back of the SUV.

"Listen, I'm sorry for your loss. Today must have been difficult for you."

He shut the hatch. "Yes and no. Your family made today easier. My father and I weren't close."

"I kind of got that, still he was your only family. You must miss him."

For a moment she didn't think he'd answer. He turned and headed up the steps to the front door, his slight limp now evident. She slowly trailed him, wishing she'd learn to keep her mouth shut.

He stopped with his hand on the door handle. "I miss knowing he was there. We weren't close, but there was a sense of connection that's gone."

He was all alone in the world. How sad. Without thinking about it she took his hand.

"I'm sorry," she said again. Impulsively she kissed his cheek.

His fingers threaded into her hair and he turned her mouth to his. "Don't be sorry for me," he said against her lips and kissed her.

CHAPTER FIVE

GARRETT'S LIPS SEDUCED Tori, starting out soft and growing firmer. He ran his tongue alone the seam of her mouth, seeking entrance, which she granted on a sigh. His heat drew her closer as the world disappeared.

The man knew how to kiss. One hand held her head captive to his mouth while the other started between her shoulder blades and slowly wandered down her spine to the small of her back, where his thumb caressed her sensitive flesh and his fingers teased the first swell of her derriere.

She melted under his expertise, arching into his hold, wanting his hands on more of her, all of her.

All thoughts of complications and incompatibility fled her mind. All that mattered was his mouth on hers. His body sheltering hers. Hands caught between them, she thrilled to the feel of the hard muscles under her fingers. There was no give to him as she ran her hands up his chest to loop her arms around his neck. She leaned into him, giving everything he demanded. And seeking a response of her own.

He pulled his lips free to tease the corner of her mouth and begin a trail of kisses that led to the curve of her neck. He bit her just short of the point of pain and she almost fell apart in his arms. But he pushed her back, held her until she gained her own balance, then released her.

She blinked up at him. Why did he stop?

"I appreciate the sacrifice you and your family made today. But never make the mistake of pitying me again, Ms. Randall." He opened the door and disappeared inside.

Still shaking with desire, she eyed the empty doorway. Feeling cheated and chastised, she folded her arms around herself. And boom. Just like that the brooding recluse was back.

Oh, yeah, no way would she ever make that mistake again.

Hands clasped behind his back, Garrett paced his office. He'd read Tori's report on the available venues for the anniversary party and he was unhappy with the results. Unfortunately Kira confirmed the information, leaving him with the choice of going substandard, over budget or out of the area. None of which was acceptable.

He walked to the window overlooking the north lot, which included the western panorama. Of the three, the only one he'd consider was the high-end hotel, but he found it hard to reconcile that decision when he was asking all his directors and departments to watch their spending.

In the distance he spotted the top gable on The Old Manor House. Tori had not repeated her suggestion of using the house for the event. She didn't have to—once mentioned it lingered out there as an option. Of course he saw the appeal of the house as a draw for the event. Seeing inside the iconic old house would ensure participation by press and industry professionals alike.

But it would be like opening a vein and exposing the wound to the world.

He'd spent many lonely years in the house that was more museum than home. Both as a child and in recent months. He'd love nothing more than to get rid of the house, but it was entitled. As if he'd ever want to thrust the albatross onto his child.

Hell, as if he'd ever have a child. That would require letting a woman close again. He'd decided the pain wasn't worth the risk.

He turned away from the view, strolled back to his desk, where he stared blindly at Tori's email.

He obviously lacked whatever was necessary to sustain a long-term relationship. His mother left. His father wanted him near but couldn't be bothered to spend time with him. Stepmothers barely acknowledged his existence. And his fiancée dumped him when he left the studio, proving she'd cared more for his status than him.

A man could only take so much rejection before he determined it wasn't worth the effort. These days he preferred short-term, no involvement associations. And he'd been too busy, too scarred up over the past year to even bother with that.

Which explained the madness of kissing Tori Randall.

It had been too long since he'd touched a woman. Or had a woman, besides a physical therapist, touch him. For a moment he'd forgotten Tori was an employee, or the next best thing. He preferred to keep professional relationships just that, regardless of how beautiful the woman.

And if he were honest with himself, surgery had given him back the use of his leg, but the Frankenstein results were an ugly reminder of what he'd been through. Not something he wanted to show off. The doctors said cosmetic surgery could clean it up, but the thought of more time under the knife turned his stomach.

Back to business, the decision on the anniversary venue finally came down to expedience. He disliked having his space invaded, but it would be the biggest draw, reach the biggest audience to turn around Obsidian's failing reputation. Yes, it would require cleaning and repairs, but it was updating that needed to be done.

With his decision made, Garrett picked up the phone to

call Lauren Randall. All things considered, he felt it best to keep his interactions with Tori to a minimum.

Looking crisp in a red skirt suit, Lauren strolled into Tori's office and sank gracefully into a visitor chair. "I heard from Garrett on the venue."

Tori sat back in her chair, arms crossed over her chest, brows reaching for her hairline.

"He contacted *you?*"

"Yes."

"Why?"

Lauren crossed her legs. "Don't you want to know what he chose?"

"We'll get to that." Tori leaned forward on her desk, pinned her sister with a narrow-eyed stare. "Did you know Garrett was Ray's guest yesterday?"

"No."

"Because it would have been helpful to have the information ahead of time."

Lauren held up both hands in a sign of surrender. "I promise I didn't know. Ray didn't say."

"Ray." Tori tapped her fingers on her desk as she contemplated her wombmate. She was hiding something. Which reminded Tori of the feeling she'd had when she saw Lauren with their host. "You two were pretty chummy yesterday. Anything you want to share?"

"About me and Ray? There's nothing to tell."

Uh-huh. She appeared her usual poised self, except for the rocking of her high heel, a tell Tori had never clued her sister into. Oh, yeah, something was there. Exactly what was hard to say. Tori thought she picked up on a romantic vibe, but it could be the same type of thing she was going through with Garrett, an attraction she had no intention of acting on.

Especially after the way he left her hanging yesterday.

Today she wondered what she'd found so attractive. A beautiful profile and godlike body were no excuse for a shadowed soul.

"So what venue did Black choose?"

"He's decided to hold the event at The Old Manor House."

"Really?" She plopped back in her chair. "It truly is the best choice."

"Agreed. Unfortunately it's going to be a lot of work. Most of the place has been closed down for years."

"He mentioned that when I drove him home last month." Tori pulled a pad toward her and started to make a list. "How bad is it?"

"Hopefully not too bad." Lauren hesitated, causing Tori to look up from her list. "I have an appointment with him tomorrow to assess what needs to be done."

She carefully set down her pen. "You have an appointment?"

"Yes."

"And Black contacted you?"

"Yes."

"What's going on, Lauren? You handle the clients, subcontractors and vendors so I understand him contacting you about his decision even though I was the one who provided the information. But I handle the site and food service. I should be the one doing the walk-through."

"When he called, he asked that I be the point of contact."

Tori blinked, her first and totally unprofessional and inappropriate reaction was hurt feelings. He found their kiss so offensive he had to disassociate himself from her? Fine. She understood completely.

After spending the remainder of Thanksgiving pretending nothing happened between them, she wasn't particularly looking forward to a repeat performance.

Except she had a job to do. And his little tantrum was getting in the way of that.

"Did you explain to him how we work?" she demanded.

"Of course I did. He didn't care. He prefers I relay information to you."

Another pinch she determinedly pushed away. She didn't have the luxury of giving in to hurt feelings. "But after the initial walk-through, I'll have access?"

Lauren shook her head. "He wants to keep the intrusion into his private quarters as minimal as possible."

"That's not going to work."

"No. It's not. What happened between you two?"

"Nothing." Lauren dodged the question about Ray; Tori figured she deserved the same privilege.

"There has to be some reason he doesn't want to work with you," Lauren pointed out.

Yeah, message received. And she'd be happy to give him his way, but she couldn't effectively do what needed to be done from a distance. And they were way too busy to play games.

"You heard Jenna and the others. He's temperamental. Who knows why the man does anything? I'm totally stumped on how we're ever going to find a match for him. What I do know is we can't let the man dictate how we conduct our business."

"True enough." Lauren lifted one fine brow at Tori. "You know what we're going to have to do."

"Oh, no." The denial came out as instinctively as the hand that flew up in a halting gesture. "It's been years since we attempted that."

"It'll be fine. We never failed to fool our target."

Tori threw up her hands. "I can't believe you're the one suggesting we trade places. You always argued against it."

"Because we were only ever fooling around and the risk was not worth the reward."

"Right, we were having fun. This is business. Black will be furious if he finds out."

"So he can't find out." Lauren leaned forward, her golden gaze earnest. "You said it, we can't let him dictate how we do our business, but we can't afford to antagonize him, either. Desperate circumstances require desperate measures."

Tori smoothed her hands down the sides of Lauren's plum business suit and followed Garrett from the front parlor to a large drawing room with attached conservatory.

So far, so good. Tori paired the pencil skirt suit with a black turtleneck sweater and black pumps, which were a good two inches shorter than anything Lauren owned. She'd swept her longer hair into a French twist and used a heavier hand with her makeup to complete the transformation.

She'd tested her impersonation by stopping at the showroom before heading to The Old Manor House. None of the kitchen staff noticed anything off. Eyeing Garrett's broad back, she continued to channel her sister. It amazed her how easy it was to know how Lauren would act in any given situation.

Tori made a mental note to remember this the next time she had to confront someone. She tended to duck and dodge. Projecting Lauren might save her from a bad haircut.

"The lines of this room are wonderful. And I love the way it opens to both the conservatory and the terrace. Having the event here will be a huge draw. We can anticipate at least three hundred people."

She continued to stroll the room. About twenty-by-forty, it would hold a good number of people, once they removed the gym equipment and some of the dated furnishings. She pushed open the terrace doors, stepped outside. The large outdoor space had been designed for entertaining. Doors also opened onto it from the conservatory.

"Nice cat." A large gray cat, very like the one she'd seen when she drove Garrett home, sunned itself on the stone balustrade. But no, Black didn't own a cat.

He joined her outside and scowled at the sleeping cat. "It's not mine."

Right.

She retraced her steps inside. "The carpet is faded here by the terrace doors. How long have the rooms been carpeted?"

"That would be stepmother number two, so about twenty years ago. Stepmother number three kept the carpet but changed everything else. That makes the drapes and furnishings about fifteen years old."

He spoke so casually, she wondered how he could be so unaffected by such drastic changes in his childhood.

"How many times did your father marry?"

"Five. His fourth and fifth wives didn't care to live in the manor, so he bought them their own homes."

"Wow. Any half or stepsiblings?" He'd said he had no other family but perhaps there was someone out there he could claim.

"No. My father didn't care for children. Will the carpet need to be replaced?"

Four stepmothers. No siblings. And a father who didn't care for children. No wonder he was so impassive. Had he known any love in his life? Hearing his history explained some of the angst lurking in his eyes.

She felt for him, but she couldn't let her feelings go beyond sympathy. Trying to reach someone who repressed his emotions was a lesson in futility. And if you did manage to get close, it just blew up in your face. Like the kiss on Thanksgiving.

Best to stay on task.

"It wouldn't be an issue if the carpeting was a paler color, but with this deep burgundy it really shows. Tori's better at these things than I am." She couldn't resist the dig. "I'll talk to her and see what can be done."

Already her mind flowed with ideas. For the party she could get a nice rug and lay it across the threshold. Or a better fix would be to cut out the faded sections and lay down tile.

"If the weather is nice, the downstairs rooms, except for the study—" where he slept "—should be all that's needed for the party. But we're talking December so there's no telling. Do you have rooms upstairs that could be used?"

A scowl lowered his brows. "The library and media room. However, I really don't want people traipsing throughout the house."

"That won't be a problem," she said in her best Lauren voice. "Security will be on hand to protect your privacy. We'll post them at the top of the staircases to help direct traffic, and we'll have one patrolling the rooms to make sure no one wanders where they don't belong."

"Staircases? There's no need for anyone to go to the third floor."

"Three hundred people," she reminded him. "We're going to need access to every bathroom in the house."

The corner of his firm mouth turned down. "Oh."

From the look on his face she knew he was rethinking his decision to have the party at the manor. His next words confirmed it.

"Maybe this is more trouble than it's worth."

"Garrett, you're out of options." Tori's gut clenched as she realized she must take a stand. *Think, Lauren,* she breathed deeply to keep the shakiness out of her voice. "The film festival starts in less than three weeks. By Arrangement has four other events we're handling for Obsidian Studios. If you want to have an anniversary party, then this is where it will be and we need to get the cleanup crews in immediately."

His shoulders went rigid. "I'm the client. I'm the one to say how it's going to be."

"No." She swallowed hard, squared her shoulders. "We contracted for the first four events. We agreed to take on the party, too, but it's not in the contract. If we can't move forward with the party starting today, then we can't continue with it. Otherwise we put your other events at risk."

Her heart pounded and her hands found the sides of her skirt again, yet she stood her ground. Lauren would have a fit at disappointing a client, but she'd support Tori's decision.

"I— We can do this, Garrett. We just need your cooperation."

"Funny you should mention cooperation."

The silky quality of his voice sent goose bumps rippling over her skin. Uh-oh. Edging away, she half turned, giving him a view of her profile.

"Shall we take a look at the upstairs room?" she suggested, deliberately cheerful. "I'd also like to see the kitchen." Putting action to words, she headed off, half hoping he wouldn't follow.

"Hold on." The hard rasp of his demand sounded right behind her. He grabbed her arm, swinging her to face him. "Tori."

Fudge sticks. Caught.

She cocked her head and raised her eyebrows in feigned confusion, hoping to brazen it out. "I'm Lauren." She pretended to wave off his error with a small laugh. "Don't worry, people make that mistake all the time.

He crossed his arms and stared down at her. "You're Tori. And I'm waiting for an explanation."

"You're mistaken—"

His mouth cut her off, his kiss a hard slant of his lips

over hers. The shock of his action threw her off stride. She placed her hands on his chest intending to push him away. Then he softened the kiss, stealing her ability to think. She sank against him, opening her mouth under his.

In the next instant she was teetering on her own feet while he strode to lean against the mantel.

"Now, Tori, tell me why I shouldn't fire By Arrangement right now."

Not trusting her legs to hold her, she perched on the bench of his weight equipment. Once seated, she glared at him. "That was unprofessional."

He arched a dark brow. "Don't get me started on unprofessional. Lauren was to meet with me today."

"You're right." Indignation fueled her recovery. "The gig is up, and I'm glad. We would never have done it if you hadn't hog-tied us."

"You're seriously blaming your lying on me."

"Yes. I can't believe you, kissing on my sister. We may look alike but we are not interchangeable." He just tapped into a twin's worst nightmare, that the guy you liked might like your sister better. Well, her worst nightmare. Lauren was a hard act to live up to.

"I didn't kiss your sister. I kissed you. Stop stalling."

Legs sturdier now, she surged to her feet. "And why do you keep doing that? You obviously have no affection for me."

His eyes blazed. "What can I say? You bring out the worst in me."

"I mean we're having a serious conversation about a difficult time in your life. I show some simple compassion. And boom you're kissing me and yelping about pity." She paced to the terrace door and back again, cautiously keeping to her end of the room. "As if anyone in their right mind would pity you."

"Are you done? Perhaps ready to talk about the real issue?"

"No." His very stillness irked her. "Because that wasn't a quick get-my-attention-I-won't-be-pitied kiss. There was tongue involved and passion. You don't kiss someone like that, then walk away and pretend it never happened."

"Ms. Randall." A touch of menace echoed in her name. "Do you want me to kiss you again?"

"Uh, no." She retreated a few steps, the backs of her knees hit the exercise bench and she abruptly sat. Darn, that could have come out stronger. She lifted her chin. "We're in a professional relationship. It would complicate things unnecessarily to inject a personal element into the situation."

"My feelings exactly. If you need to hear me admit I like kissing you, the answer is yes. It's the reason I asked Lauren to be my point of contact with By Arrangement."

"Oh."

"And as we both agree a personal relationship is not an option, we've managed to spend a lot of time accomplishing nothing. Perhaps we can now get down to business."

Still reeling from his admission, it took a moment to catch up. She stood and straightened her jacket with a tug.

"I wouldn't say nothing. We understand each other better now."

"You think so?" That dark eyebrow took another trip up his forehead.

"Of course. Communication is important in any relationship, personal or professional. We'll be better equipped to deal with each other moving forward."

"If we move forward. I still don't know why you were masquerading as your sister."

"We're small at By Arrangement. My sister and I each have a role to play." Okay it wouldn't do to remind him Lauren had already explained the way they worked. How did she put this so he'd understand and still keep By Arrangement under contract? "Would you ask one of your accountants to edit a film, or vice versa?"

"Of course not." He rubbed a hand across the back of his neck. "They're different skill sets."

"Exactly, but that's what you're asking of Lauren and I. We can cover for each other short-term, but to be our most effective, we each need to stick to our strengths. Especially when we're as busy as we're going to be over the next few weeks. Besides the film festival, we have three other events in December. Lauren has vendor meetings all day going over the logistics for all of the events. It was important she take those meetings."

"Why didn't she just schedule me for another day?"

"Because we can't afford to lose another day." She drew in a deep breath, let it out slowly. "Sorry. We didn't want to blow off your request, but we couldn't honor it, either."

"So you became Lauren so she could be in two places at once."

"And because this is what I do. I needed to see what we're working with here. I oversee the site and the food. It's my job to evaluate the site, conceive the design and calculate what's needed to pull off the event."

She blinked up into his silver gaze. Her passion had driven her across the room until she stood right in front of him.

He contemplated her for a moment, then moved to the open terrace doors and stood, hands clasped behind him as he stared outside. She held her position, allowing him time.

"So in your professional opinion you feel the manor would work for the anniversary party?"

"I think it would be freaking fabulous." She walked over until she faced his profile. "It would be the event not to miss. But I meant what I said, if you choose not to have it here, By Arrangement can't handle the event. We can't afford to spend any more time spinning our wheels."

"But you believe you can whip the manor into shape in the time we have?"

"What I've seen is mostly cosmetic. The house has been kept up, the structure is sound. So yes. If we get started today, I can get it done."

He turned his unreadable gray eyes on her and gave a brief nod. "Do it."

"Yeah." Relief and excitement lit her up inside. She threw her arms around him in a big hug. "You won't be sorry." Ideas rolled off her tongue as she searched for her notebook. She found it on the exercise bench, retrieved it and kicked off her shoes before heading for the stairs. "I want to see the upstairs and the kitchen. Then we'll go through each room again and go over the specifics."

Behind her, his muttered "I'm already sorry" barely registered.

CHAPTER SIX

"THIS IS NOT working, Ms. Randall," Garrett stated, the cell connection bringing his irritation up close and personal. "There are too many interruptions. I need you on-site."

"That's not going to happen. Our schedule is insane right now." She keyed her screensaver up in order to give Garrett her full attention. "What's the problem? The dust will settle down once they get through all the rooms." Saints have mercy, it had only been two days.

"So you said." Exasperation echoed down the line. "The carpet people came out today and there's hardwood under the wall-to-wall carpet."

"Really?" That could be good news for their schedule. "What shape is it in? Are you going to be able to use it?"

"Possibly. I'm told it may take longer to resurface than to lay the new tile you suggested, which brings me to my point. You need to be on-site. We lost half a day's work while the carpeting staff waited for me to arrive home and direct them. We can't afford that kind of delay."

"I'll come by tomorrow and talk to the contractor."

"Yes, and ten minutes after you leave they'll be calling me again. I, too, have a busy schedule."

"Maybe you could work from the house for a few days?" Silence met her suggestion, then a grinding noise.

"I am not a designer, Ms. Randall. This was your sug-

gestion. I expect you to handle it." This time the silence
was followed by a trill announcing the call ended.

Aggravating, demanding man. Nothing was easy with
him. She activated her computer and scanned her schedule. She wedged the promised trip to the Old Manor into
an already packed day. Then she turned her attention to
the preview event scheduled in a few hours.

She'd probably be having the same conversation in person. Garrett was nothing if not tenacious. Strangely, she
looked forward to it.

"Red carpet is active." Lauren's voice came through the
headset. It meant they had three hours until the *Tattoo
Murders* postpremiere party.

Tori passed the information on to her kitchen staff. They
were working off-site. The beautiful old theater had the
seats to accommodate a large audience, including the balcony section where the postparty would be held, but there
was no kitchen to speak of, so the food would arrive thirty
minutes prior to the end of the screening.

Until then, she and Lauren were on-site supervising
the setup of the balcony into an ultrasuave lounge. Black
leather sofas and chairs created conversation groups while
chrome cocktail tables added a reflection of light. Three
bar stations provided easy access to liquid refreshments.
Waiters and waitresses would carry trays of food.

Large banners showing a portion of the skull tattoo featured in the movie spanned the length of the theater. Two
cupcake displays were already in place and picked up on
the skull theme. Temporary tattoos matching the movie
were available throughout.

For the preevent waitresses wearing the tattoos were
ready to serve iced water and freshly popped corn. A candy
table featured all kinds of theater delights.

Tori stole a pack of Sweet Tarts as Lauren strolled up.

"We should see the first guests in a few minutes." Her sister shook her head when Tori offered a Sweet Tarts candy. "The space looks spectacular. The way the banners curve with the theater really make the tattoo come alive."

"We're ready here," Tori assured her. "I'd like someone from security to keep an eye on the bar stations in case anyone decides to help themselves."

"I'll take care of it." Lauren selected a red Cherry Vines candy, took a bite. "Garrett will be here tonight."

"Probably. He didn't mention it when he called to complain about the cleaners. They only started two days ago and I've already gotten three calls from him. Today it was the carpet. Yesterday the dust. Tomorrow it'll probably be the sun is shining too brightly through the clean windows."

Lauren laughed. "He's not that bad."

"Nearly." Tori shook her head. "He's nervous about this project, so he's twitchy."

"Or he likes talking to you," Lauren suggested.

Tori placed her palm on Lauren's forehead. "Are you sure you're feeling okay?"

"Ha-ha. If we're going to do the matchmaking thing, we should take advantage of tonight. Try to observe him as he interacts with the women attending."

"If? Do we have a choice?"

"We could tell Jenna and the others that we've decided we can't put one client's needs before another's."

"I vote for that option." For some reason Tori found the idea of matchmaking for Garrett more and more distasteful. "Do you think they'll accept that?"

"I'm not saying they'll like it." Lauren straightened a dish on the table. "But what can they do?"

"Make our lives miserable until after the wedding. Cancel their contracts. Bad-mouth our business." Tori outlined the worst-case scenarios. She liked the three women, they'd become friendly, but bottom line they were clients, not friends.

"The last is what concerns me. We can't count on friendship when it comes to our business." Lauren voiced Tori's thoughts. "We've reached a new plateau. We can't risk what we've achieved."

"Obsidian is the bigger contract." Tori swept a hand out, encompassing the current venue. "We don't want to antagonize Garrett."

"You've already done that, with the whole trading places thing."

"Me?" Tori planted her hands on her hips. "It was your idea."

"Yeah, but you got caught," Lauren taunted. "How did he know?"

Tori wondered about that, too, but hadn't thought it very smart to ask. "We were talking about whether we were going to match him up or not. I vote we don't."

"Really?" Lauren surveyed her, an odd look in her eyes. "I vote we do. I'm not happy about it, but it's not like we'd be hurting him, just helping him find love. And hopefully he'll be none the wiser."

"I suppose," Tori conceded. She felt cheated, as if she'd had a treat dangled in front of her then yanked away. "I'll keep a look out tonight, but it won't be easy while we're working."

"What are you talking about? We were working when we paired up both Jenna and Cindy."

"Here come our first guests," Tori noted with relief. "Let's rock this event."

The postpremiere party for *Tattoo Murders* was in full swing when Garrett sprung free of the theater. A reporter from one of the entertainment magazines had waylaid him.

Word traveled fast in the film industry, and he'd heard of the changes Garrett mandated on current productions.

Garrett shrugged it off as the normal tightening of the reins with the takeover of new leadership. Which was true as far as it went. No need to advertise the fact his father had gotten too lax in his policies.

A waiter offered him an option of appetizers. He chose a stuffed mushroom and headed for one of the bars. Glass in hand, he made a circuit of the room. People hailed him from all sides. He nodded, shook hands and exchanged quips.

The venue was perfect. Everyone raved about being able to walk right into the party. Tori's idea. Garrett must admit he appreciated the convenience.

Overall By Arrangement had done a great job. The food was tasty, the bars were well-placed, the seating comfortable while allowing for flow of movement and the movie graphics were tasteful and fun. Many people sported the temporary tattoos.

It all seemed effortless, but he spotted Tori directing a waiter to collect empty glasses from a table. His gaze swept over her. She wore a black sheath dress with interesting cutouts in the asymmetrical neckline. Her long blond hair fell over one shoulder in a river of molten gold, drawing attention to the ivory perfection of her neck.

She probably thought she faded into the background. Not so. The black fabric faithfully hugged every subtle curve. He noted more than one male head turn in her direction as she wandered the length of the room.

He continued to move, following in her wake only because he'd already been headed in the same direction. He made a point of congratulating the director and stars of the movie but avoided any in-depth conversations. Once he spoke with Olivia Fox, the female lead, he'd consider his duty met.

He spied her standing at a cocktail table with Jenna, Vick and Tori. He stopped for another drink, then strolled up behind them.

"I was hoping we'd see Black with someone tonight," Vick was saying.

"Me, too." Fox sounded disappointed. "I now know what you were talking about. Getting through security on the lot is worse than the airport. It's a pain."

"Sorry," Tori said. "We're really busy, and we don't actually have a lot of access to him."

What was this about? Why would Tori apologize?

"Maybe there's someone here tonight?" Vick suggested. The two actresses moved to flank Tori while they all looked down the length of the room. "What type does he like?"

Type? His gaze followed theirs, perusing the beautiful people of Hollywood. A bad feeling brewed in his gut.

"It doesn't work like that," Tori advised her companions. "It's not like there's a questionnaire or anything. It's more instinctive."

"Well, whatever it is—" Olivia turned a pleading moue on Tori "—do something. Black seriously needs a woman to mellow him out."

"Before Christmas would be good," Vick added. Tori and Olivia both glanced at her. She shrugged. "Just saying. It would make a nicer holiday for everyone."

He took that as his cue. "Good evening, ladies."

The three women jumped and swung to face him.

"I hope you enjoyed the movie," he said pleasantly. "Ms. Fox, you were particularly moving in the role of Grace."

"Thank you, Mr. Black." Olivia Fox quickly recovered. "I hear there's a lot of award buzz for the movie."

"I've heard whispers, as well. We'll keep our fingers crossed, shall we?"

"Fingers and toes, as my mama would say." Olivia's smile proved her sultry role drew from true life.

"You'll have to invite her to the Academy Awards," he proposed. "Perhaps she'll bring us luck."

"Oh, so family is allowed at the awards show," Vick mused in an odd tone. "Good to know."

He ignored that. "Ms. Randall, if I can have a word."

"I should really get back to work." Tori began backing away.

"No." Garrett caught her arm. "You really should talk to me."

"We'll let you two chat." Vick waved as she walked away.

"Bye, Tori." Olivia strolled away with Vick. "Good luck with that project."

He drew Tori to an alcove half-hidden by the long flow of curtains and one of the tattoo banners.

"Garrett, I've already taken a break to chat with Jenna and Olivia," Tori protested. "If this is about the house, I put it on my calendar to stop by tomorrow morning at ten. I really should go. Lauren will be looking for me."

"It's your little chat with the girls that I wish to talk about." He crossed his arms over his chest and eyed her expectantly.

She closed her eyes on a pained expression. "You heard."

"About the woman intended to mellow me out? Yes." He lifted both eyebrows in inquiry. "I'm waiting for an explanation."

"I can explain. But before I do, let me make it clear it's all your fault."

"My fault?" He couldn't help it, the corner of his mouth twitched. He pressed his lips together to quell the inappropriate humor. "How is that possible?"

"You're the one who's made life on the set tough for everyone."

His brows slammed together. "What are you talking about? What do you have to do with my film sets?"

"Nothing!" she exclaimed as if he'd proven her point. "And I don't appreciate being put in this position."

"Enough with the two-step," he demanded. "I want to know what the hell is going on."

"Tori." Lauren appeared around the tattoo banner. "The kitchen is looking for you." She turned to him, flinching slightly as she recognized him. She pasted on a smile as she greeted him. "Hello, Garrett, I'm sorry to interrupt. Perhaps I can help you while Tori takes care of business?"

"That's okay." Oh, these two were good, their choreography nearly flawless. "Tori will be stopping by the house tomorrow morning." He snagged Tori's amber gaze and sent a clear message. "I'll get my answers then."

Tori arrived at The Old Manor House earlier than planned. She didn't want Garrett to think she was running scared. She'd decided to be completely honest with him about the matchmaking situation.

It may well surprise Garrett to know, but she preferred to be truthful. Which probably explained why she was off her game with him. Circumstances had forced her into playing games she generally avoided.

Best to just come clean and ask for his cooperation. After all, it would benefit him and his studio to be friendlier to the industry professionals using his services.

Right. He owned the studio. It wasn't as if he needed Jenna's and Olivia's goodwill.

Tori refused to let the dynamics deter her. Instead she focused on the house. As she walked through the downstairs rooms, she understood how the chaos could be daunting to Garrett. The necessary destruction before reconstruction tended to be quite messy. And loud.

She spoke to the cleaning and construction supervisors. Gave both a stack of her cards, and instructed all calls be directed to her. She would determine if Garrett needed to be consulted. The men nodded their agreement.

"What do you want to do with the flooring?" The cleaning specialist drew her attention to the hardwood floors unearthed near the terrace doors.

The three of them examined the area. The flooring specialist had polished up a section to give an indication of how the finished flooring would look. The grain in the wood gleamed in the late morning sunshine.

"This is expensive wood, meant to endure," the specialist said. "It was a crime to cover it up. I advise pulling up the carpeting and refinishing the floors."

She agreed with his assessment, but the construction supervisor pointed out the time constraints and the possibility of complications. "The floor appears sound, but you never know what you'll find. With your deadline I suggest going with the tile you originally wanted or polishing this section. The problem is all other work has to stop when you're laying down the varnish or you risk a messy finish."

"Let's go with the hardwood in this section, and I'll talk to Mr. Black about completing the job after the party."

The men nodded and went back to work.

There'd been no sign of the man himself, so she knocked on the door of the room he'd been staying in downstairs. There was no answer, so she peeked inside. The room was empty. A twin-size bed was made and everything appeared neat and tidy, except for the dust on every surface. A garment rack full of clothes stood in the corner and a lovely mahogany desk had been pushed against the wall. No personal effects graced the space.

Tori backed out and headed upstairs, looking for the

master suite. She'd managed only a glimpse on her previous tours. Maybe if she gave Garrett a nice oasis away from the construction zone, he'd deal better with the work being done. She had plenty of money to work with. He'd given her a generous allowance for the transformation, financed from his personal account. She had a separate budget from the studio for the party.

She checked out some of the other rooms, seeing what furnishings she might switch up and a plan began to form. Garrett found her at the kitchen table making notes for the crew.

He came in the back door, hesitated upon spying her, then continued into the room to set his briefcase on the big butcher-block table.

"Tori, thanks for waiting for me."

She glanced at the clock over the stove. Ten-thirty. Excellent. She loved checking items off her to-do list. Today she felt very productive. And if he saw himself as late, that only worked to her advantage.

"No problem." She rose to get him a cup of coffee from the pot she'd brewed. A teaspoon of sugar and a splash of cream later, she set the mug in front of him and resumed her seat. "Congratulations. Great reviews on *Tattoo Murders*."

He looked from her to the coffee and back again before pulling out a chair and sitting across from her. She'd obviously thrown him with the pleasantries.

"Yes. It looks like your friend Olivia has a good chance at the accolades she covets." He sipped and settled back in his chair. "Now tell me what the hell is going on."

Oh, yeah, his patience was at an end. She drew in a deep breath, blew it out over her coffee.

"Lauren and I are matchmakers." She stated it baldly, not trying to soften the news.

He rubbed his temple. "I thought you were event plan-
ners."

"As it turns out, we're both." She calmly detailed the
events that led up to last night. "So you see, By Arrangement is just trying to make everyone happy."

"By pimping me out?" It was the softness of his words
that told her of his feelings more than the coarseness of
them.

Her chin went up. "There's no need to be crude. Their
motives may be selfish, but all anyone wants is your happiness. Is that so bad?"

He shoved the coffee aside so hard liquid spilled over
the edge. "I don't need anyone to find me a woman."

The vehemence of his response spoke volumes. She
asked softly, "Don't need or don't want?"

"Both. Neither." Blunt fingers plowed through dark hair,
mussing his neat appearance. He pushed away from the
table, paced to the counter.

The uncharacteristic display revealed a depth of emotion beyond annoyance at simple matchmaking. It sparked
a memory of something she read when she researched him.

"I read on the internet you were engaged at one time."

He tore off some paper towels and returned to the table
to clean up the spilled coffee, all without answering.

"Obviously you don't have a problem committing." She
chipped away at his reserve.

"Please desist. Your friends are wrong. I have no need
of a woman in my life at the moment." He moved to throw
the paper towels away. "You can consider any request to
the contrary as unnecessary."

"Sorry, it doesn't work that way," she informed him.
"As you saw last night, the girls are looking for results."

"Too bad—" he shot back "—because I'm not giving
you any information to help find this paragon of a woman."

"We don't need it." Gathering her composure, she settled back in her chair and reached for her mug. "That's not how Lauren and I work. We feel it."

"Feel it? Like an electrical buzz?" He dropped back in his chair. "That must hurt."

"Very funny." She leaned forward on her elbows. "Tell me what happened with your fiancée."

"No." His arms crossed over his chest, a firm barrier against further intrusion. "Tell me what you're going to do about the house."

"Already taken care of." This was proving more difficult than she anticipated. And the fiancée was the key. She just needed him to open up a little. "Did you break it off or did she?"

"None of your business." He failed to relent. "What arrangements did you make for the house?"

"I spoke to the crew supervisors. They know to call me with all questions. I told them to leave the carpet and go with the hardwood floor over the tile. There's no time to varnish the whole room before the party, but you should consider finishing the job after the event."

"I'll think about it," he said.

"Good. I asked them to bring in a second cleaning crew, so the dust issue should be resolved soon."

He nodded and relaxed enough to drop his arms and lean on the table. "Obviously being on-site was helpful. I told you, you're needed here."

Bingo. He needed something and so did she. She smiled and planted her forearms on the butcher-block surface so only a few inches separated her from his pale gray gaze.

"I'll try to come by every couple of days if you agree to go on a few dates."

His eyes narrowed. "Absolutely not. You're lucky I'm not canceling our contract. First you pretend to be your twin and now you've gone behind my back to play matchmaker. I don't care for liars. Tell me why I don't fire you right now."

"Because you're too honorable to blame By Arrangement for something beyond our control." She responded honestly and without hesitation. Garrett may grouse but he was fair. In fact, he seemed more grim than usual. She glanced at her watch, after eleven. "And because it's too late to get someone to replace us. Face it, we're stuck with each other."

"Maybe." He bit out the concession. "But this project was your idea. I expect you to hold up your end of the agreement."

"Are you hungry?" She rose and checked out the refrigerator, saw the makings for sandwiches. "I am handling the renovations." She carried her cache to the table, went to the drawers for a knife. "I'll deal with the calls. But you know how heavy our schedule is. I can't promise to get by more than every few days."

"That's blackmail."

"Unfortunately it's reality. I know as a director and as president of Obsidian Studios you prefer order and control in your business dealings, but coordinating events is a matter of planning and damage control. We have to be on top of every detail to offset the inevitable disaster.

"Come on," she urged, layering meat and cheese onto wheat bread, "just five dates. It will do wonders for your reputation. You know Jenna and Olivia aren't just complaining to Lauren and me."

"Damn it," he muttered, recognizing the truth of her statement.

"It's only a few hours of your time." She pressed her advantage. "And who knows, you may actually meet someone." She slid a sandwich in front of him, started making one for herself.

"Highly unlikely." He eyed her as he took a bite.

"Can't you give it a chance?" A bit of mustard smudged her finger and she licked it off. His gaze followed the movement of her tongue. The blaze of heat in his eyes when they lifted to hers sent a wave of awareness shivering down her spine.

Ignoring her inappropriate reaction, she turned her attention to her sandwich, carefully cutting it into quarters, a habit left over from childhood. She kept half and put the other two pieces on his empty plate.

"You can set your own terms," she offered.

"Now you're suggesting fake dates?" His tone dropped several degrees.

"No." The word reflected her shredding patience. "It may surprise you, but I prefer honesty, as well. But you can have a say in the where and when."

He finished off another quarter sandwich while he thought about it. "Two dates and you come by twice a day."

She gnawed her lower lip. This was going to play havoc with her schedule. But she really had no option. She practically felt Lauren prodding her along. A good thing because her twin would have to do her part to help.

"Three dates and once a day," she countered, crossing her fingers for good luck.

His jaw clenched but he gave a brief nod. "I get to set the terms."

"Of course." Thank goodness. She reached for her electronic pad. "What are your terms?"

"No wannabes. Only established women."

"Okay." She nodded as she noted it down. "That makes sense. What else?"

"Public events only, no one-on-one dates."

"But—" Her protest cut off midsentence when she met his implacable gaze. "Public events only," she confirmed.

"And you have to be somewhere nearby to save me if things get unbearable."

Her fingers stilled. The thought of witnessing Garrett on his dates held little appeal. In fact everything in her objected to the very notion.

"Is that really necessary?"

He pinned her with granite-hard eyes. "It's a deal breaker."

She gritted her teeth and finished the notation. "Is that all?"

"For now. Except I want this done by the end of the year. I don't want it hanging over me."

"Agreed." The sooner the better suited her just fine. The chore of finding him a woman got more distasteful by the minute.

Two days later Tori completely understood Garrett's frustration with the renovations. Once she arrived at the house, she got sucked in and found it difficult to get away. With so much to be done in such a short amount of time, hundreds of details needed to be dealt with or approved. Her schedule was completely disrupted.

She glanced out the library window at the light rain currently delaying the outdoor work. With any luck it would end soon, allowing the landscapers an opportunity to make up for lost time. The gardens were in need of pruning, then a few small repairs, cleaning, sanding and painting. Last came the lights and decorations. For now she put them to work in the conservatory.

A light knock came at the open door. Maria, a lovely Latina woman in her early thirties and lead on the bedroom crew, stood framed in the doorway. "Ms. Randall, the master suite is ready for your walk-through."

"Thanks, Maria." Tori followed the woman from the room. "I'm anxious to see how the changes look."

"The room is *muy bien*," Maria advised. "Cleaning

helped a lot, but your suggestions make it more current and masculine. Señor Black will be happy, I think."

"Let's hope so." Tori really needed a win with Garrett, especially as she had news on his first date.

The room didn't disappoint. Garrett was a bit of a minimalist so she'd kept the furnishings and knickknacks to the basics. A tufted screen in dove-gray velvet outlined in black with asymmetrical points on the ends, lending it an Art Deco feel, stood as headboard to a pedestal bed. A large black area rug with gray swirls covered the floor. Warmth came into the room via the dark wood dresser and matching bedside tables she'd found in a spare room. Touches of royal-blue added a bit of color. The art was understated and soothing.

Best of all, the bed, heaped with a down comforter in steel-gray and plump pillows in black coverings, made you want to dive headfirst into slumber. The retro elements along with the modern art and bedding made the room both relevant and comfortable.

"It turned out as you wanted, *si?*" Maria inquired.

"Yes, it's perfect." Tori looked into the bathroom, saw that it sparkled. "Mr. Black will be very pleased. Thank you." She moved into the hall. "And the other rooms?"

"Cleaned, as you requested," Maria replied. "Including the study downstairs. It has been converted back to an office."

"Excellent." Tori made a quick tour. Satisfied with the results, she sent Maria and her crew upstairs to continue with the cleaning and polishing. Tori collected her laptop. She had an appointment and then she wanted to swing by her place before coming back here to talk with Garrett. Turned out he was right after all.

Garrett entered The Old Manor House through the kitchen. He set his briefcase on the table, tossed his jacket over the back of a chair and went in search of Tori. Her car in the drive indicated she was here somewhere.

He found her in the study.

"What are you doing in here? Where are my things?"

He'd put up with a lot from this woman. For some reason her quirkiness appealed to him. He never knew what to expect next. It was like a good movie, right when he thought he had things figured out, there was a new twist. But this was going too far.

Not even the play of the late afternoon sun in her blond hair offset his anger.

"Garrett." She sprang up. "Good, you're home."

"I asked you a question," he stated.

"Come with me." She walked around the desk, his ire blipped as he admired the swell of her breasts in a bright red sweater. "I have a surprise for you."

"I don't like surprises," he said for the sheer principle of it. He preferred order and discipline. Tori lacked both. How she managed to pull off the spectacular events she did baffled him. As did his irrational fascination with her dimples.

She laughed and tugged him along. "Oh, boo. Everyone enjoys a good surprise. Trust me, you're going to like this."

"I already don't like it." Okay, he did like the way her hips gently swayed in tight black jeans as he followed her up the stairs. "These rooms are closed up. The dust downstairs may be bad, but these rooms are worse."

"Not anymore." With a dimpled smile, she pushed open the double doors to the master suite. "I had all the rooms cleaned. We'll be using the bathrooms up here. It seemed smart to just clean everything." She waved him inside. "For you. Up here you'll be out of the chaos of the renovations, have your own personal bathroom and won't be squeezed into a twin bed. Your leg hasn't seemed to bother you lately, so I hope the stairs won't be a problem."

"I can handle the stairs," he asserted, pleased she didn't feel the need to coddle him. Self-conscious of his weak leg, he'd been afraid his fall would cause her to treat him as an invalid. She never did.

Perhaps that's what appealed to him, beyond the dimples and heart-shaped derriere.

"Excellent."

He took in the inviting bed, noted the Art Deco feel. He enjoyed the black and grays, the touch of blue. "You made changes."

"A few. To freshen it up." She stayed by the door while he toured the room. "I hope you like it."

Freshen? He supposed that was a nice way of saying "purge memories." He appreciated the gesture. "I might be able to live with this surprise."

"Good. Because I have another one." She dazzled him with a smile, flashing that alluring dimple.

"Another what?" He wandered to the window, pretended interest in the view to avoid temptation.

"Another surprise," she clarified. "It turns out you were right. Someone is needed on-site during the work."

"Finally. I believe that's the first sensible thing I've heard you say."

"Very funny."

He thought so. The corner of his mouth tugged up. "So does this mean you'll be stopping by more often?"

"No, it means I'm moving in."

CHAPTER SEVEN

GARRETT LAUGHED. A rare occurrence, one she'd enjoy if it weren't at her expense. She crossed her arms and sent him a disgruntled glare.

The laughter faded to be replaced with an appalled expression. "Oh, come on. You aren't serious."

"It makes perfect sense." She defended her decision. "If I work from here, I can actually accomplish something."

"So work from here," he agreed, advancing on her. "It doesn't mean you have to move in."

"I've spent the last two days working here and I've got nothing done."

He spread his arms out, gesturing to the room where they stood. "You got more done in two days than I did in twice the time."

"But I got nothing else done. Juggling home, the showroom, the manor and appointments has been impossible. If I make this my base, I can get things going in the morning and I'll be here to check on the progress between trips to the workshop and appointments."

"It's inappropriate."

"How sweet of you to worry about my reputation. But this is the twenty-first century, Garrett. No one will care."

"I care."

For a split second her heart bloomed at his words, but

she quickly corrected herself. His concern was for his own comfort, which was much easier to ignore. "Since you're office is in the library, I've set up in the study. You'll never know I'm here."

"That's highly doubtful."

Okay, no missing the scorn there.

"We'll be on two different floors," she pointed out. "We don't even have to see each other."

"You got rid of the bed in the study." He tossed the words at her.

"The new sofa can be converted to face either direction or go flat into a bed. It's really quite cool. And if you do have a bad spell, you'll have a bed downstairs." She held up a hand. "After I leave, of course."

He shook his head. "Tori, you can't stay here."

"Garrett, I really have no choice if we're going to make this work. Now, you need to change your clothes. Something warm and casual. I'll meet you in the kitchen in ten minutes." She twirled and headed for the stairs.

"Where are we going?" floated after her, and then, "I need a shower."

"Fifteen minutes," she called.

And hoped it was enough time to get her calm back. The look in his eyes when he said she couldn't stay almost singed her eyelashes. She'd wanted to throw herself into his arms and prove they'd do all too well together.

Common sense came to her rescue. Because the flash of delight she'd seen on his face when she revealed her surprise exposed a vulnerability she couldn't ignore and wouldn't exploit. Too easily memories of despair and betrayal surged to the surface, reminding her of what happened when she reached out to a wounded soul.

No. Singed eyelashes or not she needed to keep her cool and her distance while she pulled off the makeover of the year.

* * *

"You brought me out to shop for a Christmas tree?" Garrett sent her a skeptical glance.

"Christmas trees," she corrected. Hooking her arm through his to keep him from escaping, she strolled into the festive lot. The spicy sent of pine filled the chilly air. "Smells wonderful, doesn't it? We'll need at least three."

"Why so many?" Little puffs of steam appeared with each word.

"Everyone loves Christmas trees." Two young boys raced right for them, Tori sidestepped out of their way right into Garrett. "Ugh. Sorry."

"No problem." But he untangled his arm to place a hand at the small of her back and direct her through the slick lot. "Be careful." He moved her around a puddle. "Everything is wet from the rain earlier. I'm surprised to see so many people here."

"Hey, nothing stands in the way of Christmas."

"So it seems." He actually appeared surprised, which made her wonder about his childhood. From what she'd read, his mother left his father and Garrett when he was three, a very young age to lose a mother. And it was probably more confusing than comforting to gain a stepmother within a few months. "Now explain why we need three."

"Each tree will create a cheerful focal point, helping to set the tone for the party. We get big impact for little effort."

"Fa la la la."

She grinned. "That's the spirit. Now we need a big tree for the foyer."

"This way." He drew her to the left. "The larger trees are at the back."

"Great." She eyed his chiseled profile. At least he hadn't bolted. "Does your family have any special ornaments you'd like me to incorporate into the decorating?"

He shrugged. "Hell, I don't know. I can't tell you the last time I had a Christmas tree."

"Surely when you were a child there were trees?" Tori couldn't conceive of a Christmas without a fully decorated tree. Her mother, the queen of holidays, always made sure they had a big, beautiful, live tree. It was one of Tori's favorite parts of the season.

"I remember some in the servants' quarters, but none in the main house." The lack of inflection in his voice told her he really had no expectations for the season.

"Oh. Was it a religious preference?" She could think of no other reason a child would be deprived of the magic of the holiday.

"No." He frowned. "My father didn't like the fuss."

"Wow, that's sad." She patted his arm. "We'll make up for a few of those years tonight."

"No need." Appalled, he sent her a quelling glance. "I'm fine."

"I don't believe that. Everyone deserves a merry Christmas. Ah, here we are, eight feet and up." She rubbed her gloved hands together as she contemplated the huge trees all lying on their sides. "Here is where we need your muscles. I need you to hold them up so I can check out their shapes."

Her request earned her another glance from piercing gray eyes, but he manfully stepped forward and hauled up the first tree, a beauty easily nine feet tall.

"We're never going to get this in the SUV," he advised her.

"No, we'll have it and the one for the terrace delivered." Circling to the left, she spotted a sparse section and gestured him to the next tree. "We'll bring home the one for the parlor."

"Why not have all the trees delivered?" He patiently held a twelve-foot Noble fir for her inspection.

The majestic tree was tall and full and beautiful. Beads of water glimmered in the overhead light. Perfect.

She clapped her hands. "This is the one."

Garrett nodded and waved an attendant over. The freckle-faced teen tagged the tree and took over Garrett's place holding the trees for their next pick.

"We need another one for the terrace, maybe not so big." She shook her head at the first one. "Too skinny."

The next was too squat. Garrett moved along with her, but stood hands in pockets, a look of disinterest on his face. She continued on task. Business first, pleasure second. She couldn't take too long or he'd lose patience. Luckily the next pick met her exacting criteria and the teen tagged it and gave them a delivery receipt.

"I love Christmas." She rubbed her hands to together. "This is really putting me in the mood. Hey, I had a great idea today. What do you think about having snow at the party? We can set up a machine so it falls onto the terrace."

"No."

She couldn't prevent a small pout. "You're not even going to think about it? Just a light snowfall, for show. We're putting heaters out there and there's the fire pit. It'll be fanciful but toasty."

"I've lived in New York. I can tell you it'll be wet, damp and mushy."

"Southern Californians will love it," she promised. "I've always wished for a white Christmas."

"It's pretty." He wasn't moved. "Until you're sitting in a puddle."

"Oh." Disappointment was sharp at the visual. "That wouldn't be good. Okay, no snow."

"Excellent decision." He verbally applauded. "Does that mean we can go home?"

"Nope. Now we look for the family tree, which will go

in the parlor." She hooked her arm in Garrett's again and headed back to the smaller trees.

"Family?" he mocked. "There's just me."

"You count." She took it as a victory when he didn't pull away. "This time I'll hold the tree and you choose. Do you prefer a Douglas fir," she asked, pointing to a bushy tree with longer needles, "or the Noble fir like the others we got?"

"I like the Noble."

"Me, too. Here we go. Six feet, that's what we're looking for." She trudged down a narrow alley of trees, reached down and grabbed one by the spine and pulled it up for Garrett's appraisal.

"That one's good," he declared.

"Nice try," she chided. "There's a big hole on this side. Remember you're looking to impress three hundred of your closest friends."

He scowled at her and shook his head. She set it down and bent for the next. After the fourth tree and catching him looking at her backside, she demanded, "What's wrong with this one?"

"It's bottom heavy."

"Bottom heavy my—"

"Wow, Mommy, that one is booiful," a young voice said with awe.

Tori looked behind her and down, way down, to a little boy with a blue knit cap on his head. He stood hands on hips staring up at the tree she held.

"You like this one?" she asked him.

His small head bobbed up and down. "It's booiful."

"Sam!" A young woman with dark hair and a baby in her arms struggled up to them. "Sam, I've told you to not run off like that."

"But, Mom, I founded the perfectest tree." Sam held his arms wide as if he'd personally conjured the tree.

The joy on his face reflected the true magic of the season. Tori's heart melted at his innocent delight.

"Oh, baby, it is pretty, but these people have already chosen it." She stood and faced Tori and Garrett. "I'm sorry."

"No need." Tori smiled, happy to inform her, "In fact, we aren't taking this tree if you want it."

The woman's pale skin pinked as she shook her head. "No. It's out of my budget. Come on, Sammy."

"But, Mom!" the boy protested loudly. "They said we could have it."

Tori met Garrett's gaze over the kid's head. He hunkered down to talk to the boy. "Sam, you need to listen to you mother. She need's you to be a good boy and help with your little sister. Can you do that?"

"But this is our tree." His mouth trembled. "Mommy wants to leave it."

"Sometimes mommy's need to make hard decisions," Garrett explained. "Getting a smaller tree might allow her to get you and your sister a nice present."

"A present?" Sam blinked.

Garrett nodded.

"I'm sorry, Mommy." Sam moved over and tucked his little hand into his mother's. "We can get another tree."

"Thank you." Sam's mother bobbed her head in appreciation at Tori and Garrett, then started to turn away.

"Actually—" Garrett's voice stopped her "—since Sam is being so good, we'd like to give him a present. If you don't mind?"

Clearly uncertain, the woman gently bounced the baby while she made up her mind. She glanced down at Sam, who stood silently at her side. Finally she shrugged. "He is being good, so okay."

"Excellent." Garrett waved the freckle-faced teen over. "We'd like to give him this tree."

"Yipee!" Sam hopped up and down.

"Oh, but," the mom protested, "it's too much."

"Please accept it." Tori handed the tree off to the teen and dusted her hands together. "Believe me, he needs to make points with Santa."

The woman gave Garrett an odd look, but a tug on her hand pulled her gaze down to her son. At his pleading expression, she gave in. "Thank you both. You're going to make great parents someday."

"Oh, no," Tori objected. "We're not—"

"Ready?" the woman supplied. "I understand. You have that newlywed glow. Enjoy your time alone. But believe me kids truly are a blessing. You made Sam very happy. For that I wish you both a merry Christmas."

Careful not to glance at Garrett, Tori decided to let it go rather than embarrass everyone with awkward explanations. "Happy holidays to you, too."

Once the small family wandered off to collect their tree, Tori confronted Garrett. "That was incredibly sweet."

He lifted one shoulder in a half shrug, his expression as stoic as ever. "He's a good kid."

"Yeah." She nodded, continuing to pin him with an inquiring gaze. Finally a hint of red appeared in his cheeks.

"And apparently I need Santa points."

She grinned. "Considering you could give the Grinch a run for his money, yes, you do. Helping to decorate your family tree will gain you more points. Now, which of these trees did you really like?"

He reached down, wrapped a large hand around the trunk of the second tree she'd held up and brought it to a stand. "This one will do."

"Garrett." She propped her hands on her hips. She didn't want just any tree. It had to be prefect.

"You said my choice." He took off for the cashier.

"Wait." She trudged after him, careful of the ground

slick with puddles and pine needles. "You said it was thin on one side."

"I'm sure your Christmas magic will hide any flaws."

"Yes, but—"

He stopped, cupped her head in his free hand and kissed her quiet.

Without conscious thought she pushed to her toes, angling closer to him as she opened her mouth under his. He sipped from her, tantalizing her with the need for more, before pulling his head back.

"Enough, darling. It's time for the newlyweds to go home."

The next morning Tori woke to a strange room awash in sunshine. She squeezed her eyes closed. Ugh. The study had east-facing windows and she'd forgotten to close the heavy drapes.

A peek at her travel clock showed the time of 6:10. Work crews would arrive at seven. She wanted to be up and dressed by the time they arrived. According to her cleaning supervisor, Garrett generally left the house just after seven.

Remembering how things got a little carried away last night, she figured if she timed things right, she could miss Garrett by giving the crews their directions for the day first. Then she'd make herself breakfast before starting on her to-do list.

Cursing the fact she'd forgotten her slippers, she shivered as she tiptoed to the bathroom across the hall.

In the parlor she spotted their purchase from the night before standing bare in the middle of the room. She'd planned on completing the decorating, but Garrett's kiss had changed her mind.

He may be aggravating, but the truth was she found his touch all too addicting. So she chose to retreat instead.

She circled the tree, still feeling the need to draw him into the holiday festivities. Sometimes the sadness in him was so strong she sensed it coming off him. No one deserved to be sad and lonely at Christmas. He may not have happy holiday memories, but that didn't mean he couldn't make some.

Tonight they'd decorate the tree.

"Ms. Randall, there's a nursery truck out front with a delivery of poinsettias," the construction supervisor advised Tori when she answered the kitchen door.

"Excellent. Please direct them to put them on the porch." While he went off to deliver her instructions, she moved to the counter. Thankfully there was fresh coffee in the pot but the cupboards were bare and the refrigerator nearly empty. She dropped a stale piece of bread in the toaster and added grocery shopping to her to-do list.

Coffee in hand, she did a walk-through with the crew bosses. The cleaning was done except where the construction needed to be completed, so Tori moved the cleaning crew to decorating. There were hundreds of white lights to go up inside, and outdoors she wanted spotlights to showcase The Old Manor House. The creepy old place was what people expected to see, so she'd leave the exterior alone, cleaned up but otherwise unadorned. Inside would be warm, welcoming, festive and elegant.

Hmm, maybe she would have the house framed with white lights for when people left the party. It would provide lighting and leave people with a jovial impression.

The large trees would be delivered today and she'd bought some pine boughs from the Christmas tree lot last night. Enough to get them started. Then she directed Maria to join her in a hunt through the attic to see if any family ornaments could be found.

Thirty minutes of dust and spiderwebs later, she gave up. There was little in the attic beyond old furnishings and a few paintings. The Blacks were not big on storing family keepsakes.

"There is nothing here." Maria finally stated the obvious.

"No." Tori dusted her hands. "That means we add it to our shopping list." She reached for her smartphone and pulled up her schedule. "I'll meet you in the kitchen in ten minutes, and we'll get started." She had the next couple of hours flagged for shopping but then she had to be at the showroom to go over the menu for tomorrow's event. "You drive, and I'll see what I can get done on the phone." She had the brilliant notion of sending the household grocery list to her head chef and sent off a text.

Garrett pulled the Spyder into the garage and cut the ignition. He ran a hand over the tight muscles in his neck. He'd been holed up in meetings with his executives all day. He was determined to have a solid strategy going into the new year.

Weary to the bone, he climbed from the car and made for the house, a house shining bright with welcome. It gave him a sense of homecoming unlike any he'd ever known.

"Don't be a fool," he muttered under his breath. "Nothing special going on here. It just means your temporary roommate is home." Yet he felt lighter as he bound up the back steps.

Inside the savory scent of meat cooking bombarded his senses, making his mouth water and adding to his odd feeling of…belonging. There was no other word for it. And repeating his little pep talk did nothing to kick-start his common sense.

Instead, he dropped his briefcase on the table and went to investigate the contents of the pot on the stove.

"Stew," Tori announced, causing him to jump as if caught with his hand in the cookie jar. The humor in her eyes told him she'd noticed the movement, but she chose not to call him on it. "I hope you're hungry."

"Smells good," he acknowledged.

"It is," she assured him as she took his place at the stove.

She stirred the pot. Leaning forward, she breathed deep and gave a soft hum of approval. The sound sent a surge of lust through his blood. Suddenly he was hungry for more than food.

"My mother's recipe," she shared, and then she winked, "with a few tweaks of my own."

He barely heard the words, so focused was he on her mouth, her soft, slightly moist lips. Her cheeky wink lured him closer until he loomed over her, his gaze locked on her plump, rosy-red mouth.

She glanced at him through thick lashes. Licking her lips, she shifted slightly to the left. "Ah, why don't you go freshen up while I dish this up? I'll give you an update on the house while we eat."

"Sounds like a plan." He backed away, realizing the luscious aroma had momentarily clouded his reasoning. The true plan was to avoid each other, but on this chilly night, after a long day, the draw of the stew overrode the annoyance of Tori's company. His last home-cooked meal had been Thanksgiving and for one crazy moment his hunger had transferred from the meal to the chef.

Garrett showered and changed in record time.

The woman talked too much. And was too damned cheerful. How did she stay so optimistic? She really did care about people. He'd seen the way she talked to the workers. She treated them as equals, listening to all opinions, making everyone feel valued while going about her own plans.

She even got to him. He preferred a steady, low-key existence yet he'd enjoyed the trip to the Christmas tree lot, took satisfaction in giving Sam a special holiday moment. The truth was Tori challenged him. She made him think, made him laugh, made him live. Too bad all he really craved was to be left alone.

He headed downstairs, rolling up his sleeves as he went. In the kitchen Tori had set the table with two servings of stew and a plate full of golden-brown biscuits.

"You didn't have to cook." As he took his seat, Garrett's stomach rumbled. Cringing a little, he met her gaze with a sheepish smile. "But I'm glad you did. This looks great."

"Tastes good, too. If I do say so myself." She boasted with a wrinkle of her nose as she reached for a biscuit. "I love a hearty stew on a cold night."

"Me, too." Though he couldn't remember the last time he had stew. No need to go into that. He dug into the food while she poured them each a glass of red wine. Silence fell as they ate.

After a few bites, she gave the report she'd promised on the ongoing projects. She talked about the progress made over the past couple of days, some of which he'd seen on his trip upstairs. The newly gleaming bannisters were decorated with greenery, crystals and lights. And the biggest of the trees now stood in the entry hall waiting to be decked out.

"It's good to see it coming along. I knew your being here would help."

"I'm glad you're happy. You'll be able to add to the progress tonight." She clicked her glass to his. "We're going to decorate the family tree after dinner."

"Oh, no." He shook his head. "I told you there aren't any family ornaments."

"I know. I scouted out the attic today. Not much up there."

"My father was never very sentimental."

"Which is why I went out and bought a slew of ornaments." Her amber eyes glittered with her excitement.

"Tonight we're going to dress the tree and next year you'll have them to use again."

She was so pleased he didn't have the heart to tell her he had no need of them. Next year he'd be back in his Santa Barbara house, back to his solitude, where a Christmas tree and happy memories would only serve to remind him of all he'd lost.

"I don't have much experience decorating," he warned her.

"Don't worry, I have lots." She rolled her eyes, then poked at the remains of her meal. "I told you my mom loved to celebrate, well she really does Christmas up big. She chooses a theme and decorates the whole house."

"Themes?"

"Yes, Santa's workshop, winter wonderland, Dickens, angels, anything Christmas related. Don't get me wrong, they're all beautiful trees. And special because we worked on them together, but my favorite ornaments were the homemade ones she kept from us kids. She pretended to grouse if they didn't fit the theme, but she let me tuck them in somewhere."

Full after two servings, he pushed his bowl aside and wiped his mouth. Her happy family memories baffled him. Her roughest recollection was having to tuck the home-made ornaments to the back of the tree?

"We had very different childhoods."

"I realize I'm lucky." She gathered the dirty bowls and carried them to the sink. "I'll do these later." Back at the table she grabbed the wine and their glasses. "Come on, we'll finish this while we work on the tree."

She sashayed out of the kitchen. He slowly followed, trailing her to the parlor, where the tree he'd chosen stood majestically in the corner between two windows. Tori set her bounty down on the coffee table and went to the wall to flip a switch.

The tree bloomed to life with hundreds of tiny lights. He stuffed his hands in his pockets, admiring the vision with just the lights. "It's beautiful just as it is."

"I agree." She came back and stood beside him to share in the admiration of the tree. "It'll look even better when we're done. You have a creative side, let it loose."

A click of a remote button had a Christmas carol singing brightly of silver bells. Tori drew him to a table laid out with gold bows, crystal icicles, glittery white snowflakes and shiny bulbs in many complimentary colors and shapes.

"Quite a collection you have here, everything but the kitchen sink."

"We don't have to use it all. Just pick what you like." She plucked up several of the melon-size gold bows. "I prefer ribbon bows to garland. I think it gives a more symmetrical balance to the tree." Suiting action to words, she stuffed the bows into the tree, then repeated the process several times. "Can you get the higher branches?"

He did as requested and quickly saw the results of her plan. Between the lights and the bows the tree seemed to glow. Next she did the same with the icicles and the snowflakes, bringing even more light into play.

Inspired by a sip of wine, he decided red would be his theme. He sorted through all the ornaments, pulling out all shades of red from the deepest claret to the brightness of Santa's cap. It didn't matter what shape it took, bird or harp, round, diamond or star, he mixed it all up and let the color make sense of it all. Occasionally she directed his hand into the depths of the tree with an ornament, adding dimension.

When she got done with the snowflakes, Tori took over putting the hooks on the ornaments and handed them to him to place in the tree.

"The red is a lovely touch. It's eclectic but traditional at the same time."

"I decided to go with theme, like your mother."

She grinned. "It's a good place to start." She curled into a corner of the couch within reach of the table so she could continue her self-appointed task. "Tell me about your mother."

The question didn't surprise him. The woman constantly had her nose in his business. Plus she'd shared family stories; she'd expect him to do the same. She'd be disappointed. On this subject he had little to say.

"Which one?" He kept his back to her as he tucked a deep red rose next to a glittering red apple.

"Let's start with your real mother." She sounded truly interested.

More evidence she cared for people. Which didn't explain why he answered, but he heard the words spilling from his mouth.

"I didn't know her very well. She left when I was three and died when I was ten."

"So young," she noted softly. "Did you see her much after she left?"

"Not a lot. Maybe once or twice a year." He said it without emotion now, but for the first time in a long time he remembered the sense of loss and betrayal he'd felt at the time. "At first all I wanted was my mother, not a stranger, be it nanny or stepmother. But it didn't take me long to realize my worth to her. I don't know if she ever loved me, but it didn't stop her using me as a bargaining chip against my father, who hated giving me into her care."

"I'm sorry," she said, reacting to the raw pain of his disclosure. "At least that shows he loved you."

There was the eternal optimist. "My father never loved anyone but himself."

"What about your stepmothers?"

"All young, beautiful actresses looking for the fast track

to stardom. He gave them that then traded them in for a newer, younger model."

"So cynical," she chastised him. "Was there no affection in your life?"

"I was well cared for. The staff saw I had everything I needed. I went to the best schools, had every advantage. My father even supported my request to go to UCLA. They have one of the best film schools in the United States."

"Your father must have been happy you wanted to follow in the family business."

"Not particularly." She kept giving his father credit for emotions he hadn't been capable of feeling. And he made sure Garrett followed his example. "He wanted me to be a mini-me of him, something I refused to do, so he didn't care what I did."

"But he made you his head of creative projects several years ago."

The article she'd read hadn't left much out.

"It didn't take."

"Why not?"

"We had creative differences."

She turned liquid gold eyes on him. "What does that mean?"

"I like projects with a good story. He wanted special effects—the bigger, the brighter, the better."

"He overrode your decisions," she guessed.

"Not for long. I quit. And got an Academy Award for my next picture. It had story as well as special effects."

She grinned. "You showed him."

He scowled and pretended to assess the tree. She read him too easily. Time to change the subject or he'd be blabbing away about how his fiancée deserted him when he left the studio.

"Do you think that's enough ornaments? I don't want to overdo it."

"You can't overdecorate a tree." She leaned forward to count the remaining red items.

In her new position the scooped neck of her sweater fell forward, providing him with the delectable view of her cleavage. He should step back out of politeness. Instead he lingered, enjoying the vision of plump breasts encased in ivory lace. His body stirred and he remembered the taste of her sweet mouth.

In the yellow sweater, with her pale skin and flowing blond hair, she absorbed the soft light of the tree so it appeared to halo her.

She resumed her former position and he stepped back, taking a moment to lecture himself on flights of fantasy and employee relations. Maybe he needed a woman more than he thought. He definitely needed something to take his mind off this woman.

"There are only six more," she stated, none the wiser of his sensual side trip. "Put them all on. Then we'll decide what to put on top."

"What did your mom use?"

"Lots of things. We had angels, Santas, bows, feathers, flowers. She always likes to make a statement, so it's big or plentiful. This is your tree, your choice."

"Hmm." He tapped his cheek with a couple of fingers while he contemplated the tree. He liked what they'd done together, the layers of light, the depth, the balance, the beauty. His tree. The satisfaction surprised him. Tonight surprised him. He actually enjoyed himself. Using his creative side felt good.

"I bet it did," Tori responded, cluing him in to the fact he'd spoken his last thought aloud. "How long has it been since your last movie?"

"More than a year. We wrapped in August. I'd started casting my next film, but the accident put it on hold."

"Because most of this year was spent in surgery and

physical therapy." She rose and came to him. He braced for her touch, and still it rocked him to his toes when she threaded her fingers through his and squeezed. Her big eyes reflected her sympathy. "And for the past few months you've been stuck on administrative duty. You've had a tough year."

"Once the studio is in shape—" it took all his control not to steal a kiss and claim all that delicate concern "—I'll be able to get back to making movies."

"So you don't intend to run the studio long-term?"

"I'll probably put in a chief executive officer. I still have to deal with some issues to redeem our reputation." Damn, he wasn't ready to discuss his plans for the studio. She got under his skin all too easily. "Forget I said that."

"Of course," she readily agreed. "I hope the studio isn't in jeopardy."

"Nothing that drastic. Tightening the reigns should solve the issue. Once it's resolved, I'll reassess my options"

"Very wise." Lifting onto her toes, she kissed his cheek. "In the meantime, try to enjoy the holidays. It's not too late to make happy memories."

Her words too closely echoed his earlier sentiment for his comfort. Christmas trees and happy memories weren't for him. Retreating a few steps, he pointed to the tree-top. "Go with a big gold bow. I like things tied up nice and neat."

CHAPTER EIGHT

TORI STRODE SOCK-SHOD into the kitchen just after seven and went straight for the coffeepot. Cup in hand, she leaned against the sink. Inhaling deeply, she closed her eyes as the rich aroma fired her salivary glands, making her mouth water. She sipped and moaned softly.

"I can leave if you prefer to be alone with your morning cup of coffee."

She whipped around. Garrett sat at the table with his own cup and a plate of dry toast. "Good morning." She slid into a seat across from him and set a file folder on the table. "Sorry, my first cup and I have a very special relationship. It's not wise to get between us."

"I'll try to remember that." He toasted her with his cup. "What's on your schedule today?"

"I'll get things started here, but I have to leave by ten to do a site inspection with Lauren." She tore off a piece of his toast, buttered it lightly. "Then it's over to the hotel to set up for your head of departments' holiday dinner. Which reminds me, what time do you want to say your remarks?"

"Remarks?" Raised brows reflected his bafflement.

"Yeah." She waved the toast about. "It's traditional for the head of the company to give some accolades or awards. What do they usually do?"

"I have no idea. There are no awards that I'm aware of.

As for accolades, there wasn't much structure this year with Dad gone and me laid up."

"Right." His comments about the studio's reputation last night explained a lot. He wasn't closing sets and tightening schedules out of a sense of mean-spiritedness, but out of necessity. "Well, your remarks should be positive, so you might want to concentrate on the studio's accomplishments through the years and finish with a statement about your vision for the future."

His chiseled lips twitched at the corner. "Sage advice. I'll take it under consideration."

"Whatever you decide, I'll give you twenty minutes just before dinner service." The need for a second cup of coffee drew her back to the pot. "That's after the cocktail hour so you should have a receptive audience. Oh, and I forgot to tell you last night, but tonight is your first date."

"What? No."

"It'll be fine. I've arranged for a car service. They'll pick up you and then Gwen and take you both to the dinner."

"It's not a good idea." He sounded slightly panicked. "This is a company event, hardly conducive to getting to know each other."

"I didn't think you wanted to get to know your dates." The reminder was for him, not her. Or so she told herself. "And it's the perfect occasion. You'll be at a table with several department heads and their spouses. You don't want to be the odd man out."

He scowled as he thought about that, and then slowly nodded. "Okay, but stay close as we agreed."

"I'm sure you'll be fine." Why was this suddenly so hard? "But in case you need rescuing, just signal Lauren or me." She pushed away from the table, wiggled her toes in her warm socks. "I have to finish getting ready. The crews should be here any minute." Using two fingers she slid the file folder toward him. "The info on Gwen is in here. You might be surprised how well you like her."

"Can't you just give me the highlights? What do your spidey senses tell you?"

She scowled while topping off her coffee mug. She ignored the reference to her matchmaking skills. Men always wanted things handed to them. As if a woman could be defined in a few words. And then she thought of Gwen and realized for a man it really was that simple. "I have two words for you, *international supermodel.*"

"How much longer are you going to be at the Old Manor?" Lauren tagged Tori as soon as she sat down at her desk.

"A few more days." She kicked off her shoes and powered up her computer at the same time. Only then did she turn her gaze on her sister. "Some of the repairs need the weather to warm up, including varnishing the hardwood."

"Well, we miss you around here. Hannah—" their executive chef "—is freaking out."

"Yeah, she's my first stop. I plan to go over the menus and shopping schedule for the next three events. Tonight we're working with the hotel catering staff. I've already called and confirmed the time, space and food choices."

Lauren checked a couple of items on her clipboard. "Great. I've talked to the meeting coordinator, too. We can start bringing in our props after three."

Tori double-checked her tablet. "That's what I have on my itinerary." She loved when a plan fell into place.

"So you'll be there at three?" Lauren asked.

"Yep."

"And everything is a go with Garrett and Gwen?"

Some of Tori's satisfaction dimmed. She shook it off. "I gave Garrett the file on Gwen at breakfast. He wasn't happy about the short notice, but he's on board."

"It was your decision to wait," Lauren reminded her.

"That's because he's never going to be happy about the dates. And if we gave him more lead time, he'd find a way to wiggle out of it."

"You know him so well?" A sparkle lit Lauren's eyes.

Tori refused to let the teasing get to her. "Sad, isn't it? If we're lucky, Gwen may be The One and we can put the matchmaking aside and concentrate on work."

"That would be lucky." There was something odd in Lauren's voice, drawing Tori's attention. She eyed Lauren curiously, but her sister gave nothing away. Which only made Tori more nervous.

"Time will tell." She dismissed Garrett and his date. It had already taken up too much of her morning. She opened the diagram of tonight's event and turned her screen to-ward Lauren. Tori relaxed as the conversation focused on work, completely missing the gleam of speculation in her twin's identical golden gaze.

Applause greeted Garrett's final comments. He breathed a sigh of relief, silently thanked Tori for the heads-up and the inspiration for his speech, and returned to his seat.

"Well done, Garrett." Irene Allan, manager of public relations, patted his hand on the table. "Your father would be proud."

Several other guests added their accolades. Garrett nodded his acceptance, feeling like a fraud. As Tori suggested, he'd kept his comments upbeat and brief. He and his father may have had artistic differences, but that didn't mean the studio lacked accomplishments over the past year. By focusing on the good, he comforted himself with the reminder he'd been truthful if somewhat optimistic.

"I'm sorry for the loss of your father." His date leaned toward him to offer her condolences, giving him a prime vantage point of her décolletage. Ample breasts swelled against the midnight-blue of her low-cut dress. Her lush curves only added to the total package of black hair, ivory skin and vivid blue eyes. She was a stunning beauty, and he'd received more than one envious glance with her on his arm.

"Thank you. It's been over a year now." He admired the view even as he acknowledged her appearance had more to do with her profession than with any desire to impress him. He supposed he could live with that.

"It was nice of him to give you a job at the studio."

The fact that her beauty exceeded her IQ, not so much, a fact he'd determined before they ever arrived at the event.

"My family owns the studio," he explained. "I inherited upon my father's passing." Obviously she hadn't read her portfolio. He looked around for Tori, frowned when he spotted her huddled with a slim man in a suit. The man seemed more interested in her blond hair as it flowed in a liquid ribbon of gold over her shoulder than in the clipboard she held.

"Wow," Gwen exclaimed. "You should do a movie about me," she said while twirling a raven tendril around her finger. "Everyone says my life would make a good story."

Good grief. It was going to be a long night.

Tori discretely followed the last of the diners as they wandered toward the dancing next door. Once the couple crossed the threshold, she closed the doors to prevent any of the guests from returning to the dining room.

"Dinner is a wrap," she advised Lauren.

"Great. I'll make a sweep through the room in a few minutes, collect any forgotten items." It was a service they always performed. Any items found would be placed on a table for people to claim on their way out of the event. "Any complaints?"

"The usual grumbles." Tori always asked for feedback

from the hotel. "Nothing serious," she muttered, her attention more on Garrett and Gwen than on her conversation.

"Getting any vibes off those two?"

The words were whispered directly into her ear. Tori jumped to find her sister so close. No use pretending she wasn't staring at their host. But then she had good reason.

"No. What about you? They seem to be getting along okay."

Garrett stood on the edge of the dance floor talking to his chief financial officer. Gwen clung to his right side, her arm linked with his, her head resting on his shoulder. He glanced down at the woman draped over him, but he faced away from her, and Tori couldn't see his expression.

"Do you think so? He looks restless to me."

"Really?" The corner of Tori's mouth ticked up. "So you're not getting any vibes, either?"

"Nope," Lauren confirmed. "No vibes for Garrett and Gwen."

Tori released a breath she hadn't known she'd been holding. And suddenly she was looking into her mirror image. Lauren stood in front of her, arms crossed over her chest.

"You seem pretty happy there's no attraction between them. Anything you want to share?"

"No!" The denial was instinctive and gut-wrenching.

Okay, yes, she'd come to think of Garrett as a friend. The Lord knew he could use a few. From what she saw besides Ray, he had no one. But any notion of a romantic link between her and Garrett was idiotic.

And yeah, the unexpected joy he'd shown in the simple task of decorating a Christmas tree and the vulnerability revealed by the few memories he shared got to her. Watching him retreat behind his facade also reminded her why he was off-limits.

If he didn't learn how to deal with his internal demons, he'd eventually implode, bringing down anyone foolish enough to care for him in the process. She knew the devastation that came with the fallout, and she couldn't—wouldn't—go through the pain of that again.

"No," she repeated more calmly. "It's just a relief to check matchmaking off tonight's itinerary so we can concentrate on the event."

"Uh-huh." Though she let it drop, the skepticism on Lauren's face warned Tori the topic wasn't forgotten. "Well, he's still the client, so we need to keep tabs on him."

As prompted, Tori kept her eye on Garrett throughout the night. She wandered through the club. Low lighting offset with spotlights of violet and gold gave the room atmosphere while flowing walls of chiffon created interesting seating alcoves. Larger couches in white leather ringed the dance floor, offering comfort between songs. The live band skillfully mixed beats between fast and slow to keep the energy high.

Garrett and Gwen twirled around the floor to a sultry melody. Turning away from the sight, Tori stepped outside.

On the terrace a tent transformed into a cigar room offered black leather seating and a black studded bar. Plants and dark wood screens made up the walls. The space was popular, in her estimation, more for the air than the cigars, but a few gentlemen puffed away.

"We could use another server in the cigar room," she said into her headset.

"On it," Lauren responded. "Sending two that way."

Lured by the beckoning hand of cool, fresh air, Tori slipped past the screen and strolled across the terrazzo decking to a poolside lounger. The fabric cushion was damp to the touch, but a headache pounded behind her eyes and the cold felt good. Kicking off her shoes, she sat down and put her feet up.

Well-placed lampposts lit the area with yellow light.

Cabanas and palm trees cast interesting shadows and steam wafted just above the surface of the water. The music from the party sounded behind her.

"I'm taking ten on the patio," she informed her sister. "Wake me if you don't see me in a few."

"Ha-ha. The servers are setting up the coffee tables. I've started closing down the alcohol stations inside. The cigar room will be last."

"Sounds good."

"I don't see Garrett anywhere. Did he leave?"

"I don't think so. He was on the dance floor a few minutes ago."

"He's not there now. Maybe the date went better than we thought, and he's taken off."

Tori's heart kicked in her chest. Setting aside her initial reaction, she tried to think logically. "Doubtful. He told me he'd be at the door at midnight to bid his guests goodbye." Tori rubbed a throbbing temple and breathed deeply of the cool night air. Juggling an event and matchmaking had never been so hard. "I'm sure he'd tell us if he changed his mind."

"Okay. Enjoy your ten."

Unable to relax with Garrett's whereabouts in question, Tori called his driver and learned he was currently driving Gwen home. Alone. Once he dropped off his passenger, he was dismissed for the night.

So much for Lauren's theory of the date.

Tori relaxed back into the cushion and closed her eyes. The fresh air worked wonders on her headache.

"Star gazing, Ms. Randall?" Garrett's deep voice came from the darkness.

She smiled but didn't open her eyes. "Reenergizing, Mr. Black."

Lauren chirped in her ear, acknowledging Garrett had

been located. Tori hummed in response and reached behind her ear to disconnect her link.

"Another successful event for By Arrangement." His voice had shifted to above her. Unnerved by the thought of him looking down on her, she opened her eyes and looked right into his silver gaze.

"I'm glad you think so." She swung around so her feet touched the terrazzo. Being grounded helped as she moved into dangerous territory. "I understand you sent Gwen home."

"Yes. She had an early appointment."

Tori bit the inside of her lip. His lack of inflection gave her no clue to how the date went. She braved a direct question. "Will you be seeing her again?"

"What do your spidey senses tell you?"

"Stop calling them that." She pushed to her feet on the protest. And still he towered over her.

He tilted his head. "What would you call it?"

Actually it was as good a way to describe her talent as any. It was his mockery she found unacceptable. "We don't call it anything. In fact, we don't generally talk about our talents at all."

"Then how come I'm in this mess?"

"Please. As if it's a hardship to spend a few hours with a beautiful supermodel."

A flash of annoyance crossed his features. He crowded her a bit. "Are you purposely not answering or is there something you're not telling me?" Intimidated but unwilling to show it, she squared her shoulders. "We get a vibe, okay. And no, we didn't feel anything between you and Gwen."

That backed him up. Not much, but he lifted his head and stared down at her. At this angle the yellow pool lights turned his eyes an interesting shade of gold. He leaned over her until she inhaled the spicy scent of his cologne and stated softly, "In that case, I'll admit it wasn't a hardship, more a waste of time."

"Gee, thanks." Faint praise, but she'd take it. Heck, high on the scent of man and spice, she'd agree to almost anything.

"Would you like to dance?"

"What?" Startled by his request, she instinctively stepped back.

"Careful." He grabbed her arm and pulled her to him.

"Goodness." A glance down showed she'd retreated to the pool edge. He'd saved her from a nasty fall into the water. "Thank you."

"I'll take that as a *yes*." Wrapping a hard arm around her waist, he drew her against him and began to move to the music.

Oh, my.

Keep your head, girl.

Unfortunately the little pep talk did little good as his warmth surrounded her. Contrarily she shivered as his heat chased the chill away. Sighing, she melted into him. Her head found the comfort of his shoulder, her breasts cushioned his chest, her body swayed to the rhythm of his.

He smelled good, felt good, moved good. She snuggled close wanting more, more, more.

The rumble in his chest and the soft rush of laughter over her ear alerted her to the danger she faced. The fact she just wanted to smile and bury her nose against him proved how far gone her inhibitions were.

The feel of his lips in her hair did the trick.

She jerked upright, stiffened her posture. Dialogue, she pulled the word from a mind gone to mush. Conversation, chitchat, something to occupy the silence between them, anything to dispel the lingering intimacy. She completely dismissed the tiny voice in the back of her head urging her to just walk away.

"Let's talk about your date." Oh, man, she cringed internally. That was the last thing she wanted to think about.

"Let's not."

"It could be helpful as I start looking for your next companion." Stupid. Why was she pursuing this?

His sigh bridged the distance she'd created, bringing his chest in contact with her breasts for a tantalizing second. "A gentleman doesn't kiss and tell."

"So you kissed her?" Okay, it was official. Aliens had taken over her brain.

"I didn't say that." His breath heated the sensitive flesh behind her ear as he leaned forward. "Why? Does it bother you to think of me kissing her?"

"What? No. Of course not." Lord, she could hear the inanity of her response. She cleared her throat. "I want you to find someone to be happy with."

"And if I'm happier alone?"

"No one is happier alone." She repeated what Shane had shared with her so many summers ago. "They just pretend to be."

He gave a harsh half laugh. "Why would anyone pretend such a thing?"

"Because it's easier. Because it's predictable and controllable. And because self-imposed loneliness hurts less than being rejected or caring for someone more than they care for you."

His whole body went stiff and he stepped away.

Her arms dropped to her sides as she stared up at him. A tick or two passed before she realized the music had stopped.

He lifted a hand, brushed his thumb over her cheek. "Thank you for the dance." Then his eyes cooled and he turned to the side. "For the entire evening, actually. The club element worked well, even if you did dial it down for the geezer crowd."

Right, back to employer-employee mode. She should be glad, but was curiously saddened instead.

"*Geezer* is a bit harsh, don't you think?" She began a search for her shoes only to have them handed to her. "Thanks." She used his arm for balance to put them on. The hard flex of muscles under her fingers reminded her how close she'd come to letting hormones overrule professionalism tonight.

"Not by Hollywood's standards. You know what they say." He placed a hand in the small of her back and aimed her toward the patio door.

"Hollywood is a young man's field?" She waved the old saying away. "I think that's less true than it used to be. Digital has been a great equalizer. And with cable and internet shows the market is wide-open. Great directors and actors only get better with time."

"Maybe I should hire you for our PR."

"Not interested. But on that note, I need to get back to work." She paused just inside the door, pondered the wisdom of her next action, but it really only made sense. "Would you like a ride home? It'll be late," she warned. "I have to stay to the end, make sure everything is wrapped up with the hotel."

He hesitated, then nodded. "Sure. I'd appreciate a ride."

The next morning Tori waited until Garrett left the house before slipping into the kitchen. Call her a coward, but walking into the house together last night had been too surreal, like a couple coming home after date night. So much so she'd almost followed him upstairs.

Obviously she needed to do a better job of avoiding him.

She poured a mug of coffee, dropped a piece of bread in the toaster and sipped while it browned. When it popped up, she buttered the toast and spread on a dollop of raspberry jam. She crunched a bite on her way to the table.

And almost choked when she saw the cover of the tabloid sitting in the middle of the table.

Lauren wrapped in the arms of Ray Donovan.

The caption read: Elusive Donovan Romances Mystery Bombshell.

OMG! Her no-nonsense sister and the bad boy director? When had that happened?

Tori recognized Lauren's dress as the one she wore at last night's event, which answered when the picture was taken. Funny, Tori didn't remember Ray being at the party.

She was so shocked it took her a minute to identify the warm sensation Garrett called her spidey sense. She remembered feeling it on Thanksgiving, too. Dim but definitely there. Wow, wherever, whenever it came to be, it was the real thing. Her mind reeled. Should she say something to Lauren or just let nature take its course?

Barely had the thought formed when her phone rang. No surprise Lauren's picture showed on the display.

"Good morning," Tori said sweetly. "I see we made the tabloids this morning."

"That's why I'm calling," Lauren said more calmly than Tori expected. "I just got off the line with Jenna. She saw the pictures of Garrett and Gwen in the tabloids and she was thrilled."

"Garrett and Gwen?" Tori flipped frantically through the magazine until she found a photo of Garrett escorting Gwen into the hotel where the party was held. The two of them made a stunning couple. Had Garrett kissed her? And why did the very notion turn her stomach?

"I cautioned her we had no control on how well the date went or whether there would be a second date."

Tori closed the magazine, which left Lauren's steamy photo front and center. "According to Garrett there won't be a second date."

"Well, we figured." Lauren sounded resigned. "In the

meantime we've made the girls happy so we've bought some time."

"Great." Tori waited a beat. When her twin didn't bring up her own notoriety, Tori prompted. "Anything else you want to discuss about last night?"

"Like what?"

"Like you and Ray Donovan in a lip-lock on the front page of *Hollywood Live.*"

Silence greeted her statement. Then she heard the click of keys on the other end of the line, followed by a sharply indrawn breath.

"Lauren?" Tori demanded. "You okay?"

"Umm. No." There was a clatter on the other end. "I've gotta go. Bye."

Tori blinked at the call-ended message on her cell.

What just happened? Clearly her sister wasn't ready to talk to Tori about her relationship with Donovan. A little hurt, she munched on her cold toast. It wasn't like Lauren to keep things from her. Then again she hadn't been too up-front with Lauren about everything that transpired at the mansion, either.

Because a few intimate moments meant nothing. No need to involve her sister over a few stolen kisses.

CHAPTER NINE

RAIN POUNDED ON the eaves of the old house. High winds whipped the moisture against the windows. Branches scrapped across exterior walls. Tori smothered a yawn. Tucked up in the parlor with a fire in the grate, lights twinkling in the tree and Christmas carols playing, she updated her files and created her to-do list for the next day.

Garrett had a late meeting, so she had the place to herself. She loved her cozy duplex and having Lauren right next door, but it was nice here in front of the fire and having a big, warm house surrounding her on such a nasty night.

Cross-legged on the couch with a mug of tea within reach on the coffee table, she fought off another yawn. Maybe she should have gone with coffee instead of tea.

She marked off most of the repairs for the Old Manor. Rain came with nightfall, but sunshine and warm temperatures over the past two days allowed the crew to complete the outdoor work and varnish the hardwood. A couple of days to finalize the decorating and they'd be ready for the party.

She sipped her tea, smiled over the mug, enjoying the mellow brew, definitely the right choice.

Boom! Crash! Darkness.

"Eee!" Tori shrieked and started. Then gasped as tea poured over her. "Sh—sugar cubes." The rumble of thunder faded while she realized a loss of electricity was what pitched the room into darkness.

She jumped up, tugging at her sweater to shake off the tea, thankfully it had cooled considerably. The flames flickering in the fireplace lent her little help. Wait, she could use her phone.

She sat and felt around. She found the mug and plate she'd used and set them on the coffee table. But no phone. Oh, dope, her computer. She felt around again, hoping desperately that she hadn't dowsed the laptop with tea. She found it on the couch, breathed easier when she encountered only a few drops on the keys.

"Thank goodness." It probably toppled off her lap when she jumped. She used the light from the screen to find her cell. Unfortunately, it read "No Service." There went the idea of calling Garrett to see when he'd be home.

Boo. She didn't want to make that call anyway. Too unprofessional, worse, too wimpy. She could do this. The danger was outside not inside. She had shelter, light and heat. Supplies if she needed them. She had it good.

"Now, to find flashlights and candles." Carrying the computer was awkward and the battery wouldn't last.

Her first step soaked her sock in tea. "Ugh." She hated wet socks.

"Pull it together," she chided. Somehow it helped to talk out loud. "You saw a flashlight in this place. Where was it?"

Kitchen, she decided. She tossed a log on the fire before making her way in that direction. Her faint hope the electricity would return by the time she reached her destination fizzled a sad death.

Lightning flashed, followed immediately by a boom of thunder. Rain pummeled the house.

Tori flinched.

Geez, she couldn't remember the last storm this bad. In

the next flash she saw the utility closet and remembered the flashlight on the top shelf. She set the computer on the counter facing the cupboard.

She didn't realize how badly she was shaking until she turned the flashlight on and the beam shook wildly over the table. Taking a deep breath, she managed to steady her grip. She shone the light around the room. Everything was neat and tidy. Steam still wafted from the spout of the tea kettle.

The normalcy steadied her nerves enough to look for candles, additional flashlights, batteries. No telling how long the outage might last. The gas stove worked in her favor if it went through the morning.

A search of the cupboards and drawers turned up nothing. Another crash against the windows drew her attention to the glass panes. She hoped they held. Time to check the mudroom.

She tried for a stiff upper lip, managed a few puckers and a bit lip. Giving up, she walked in her damp socks to the back door. The mudroom held the washer and dryer. A long folding counter with cupboards underneath ran two thirds of the room on the opposite side.

Tori found a box of candles, wooden matches and batteries. Unfortunately the wrong size for her flashlight. She carried her cache to the kitchen table.

She lit two of the stubby candles and set them on either end of the long butcher-block table in cereal bowls. The flickering glow gave light and a faux sense of warmth to the room. She shut down the computer to conserve the battery and contemplated her next move. Suddenly the big house felt cold and lonely.

The very real heat of the fireplace drew her back to the parlor. The fire and the candles made it cozy. If she discounted the oppressive darkness surrounding her.

Wrapped in the throw from the back of the couch, she

took off her damp socks and tucked her feet into the fleecy softness, prepared to wait for Garrett.

She stared into the fire, watching the flames. In perpetual motion, the brilliant oranges, yellows and reds flowed in a wild dance of beauty and destruction. The mesmerizing show almost distracted her from the unnerving creeks and groans of the old house, the unrelenting sounds of the storm.

Rain pounded the roof and lashed the glass while branches continued to buffet the house. Growing antsy with nothing except the storm keeping her company, she dug up her iPod put in her earphones and zoned to a country mix.

The unexpected feel of a hand on her shoulder spooked a shriek from her. She jumped to her feet, brandishing the flashlight, ready to fight off any specter. The big black shape looming behind the couch fit the description.

"Tori, stop," a gravelly rasp directed. "It's me, Garrett."

"Garrett?" She aimed the light at him. "Thank God." She launched herself into his arms, climbed right over the couch and threw her arms around his waist. "I'm so happy to see you."

"Hey." He drew her close so her head rested under his chin. She heard the reassuring thump of his heart under her ear. A large hand ran over her hair in a soothing motion. "Are you okay?"

"I am now that you're here." She breathed in his scent, comforted by his presence.

"It's a hell of a storm." He continued to pet her, his fingers feathering through the ends of her hair before starting at the top again. "Lightning hit a power pole. Half of Hollywood Hills is out."

"Do they know when it'll be back up?"

"No word yet."

The time to let him go had come. She knew it, yet she

clung to him. He was alive and warm, strong and steady, everything she'd craved while struggling alone. She needed a few minutes to let the tension of the past couple of hours fade away.

"I'm sorry you were afraid." His breath blew over her temple, lifting stray strands of hair.

His nearness made her feel safe, cherished. His demand for perfection may occasionally be annoying but tonight he was her rock. Still, his words jerked at her pride. And a drop of water hit her cheek. Reluctantly she pushed away from him, her fingers sliding over firm abs. Very reluctantly.

She cleared her throat, lifted her chin. "Unnerved maybe, but I handled myself."

"I can see that." He ran a large hand through his hair and it came away wet. "The candles were a welcome sight in the kitchen."

"Goodness, you're soaked." She circled the couch, grabbed up the dish towel she'd used as a teapot cozy and tossed it to him. "This should help."

"Thanks." He rubbed the cloth over his head, leaving his hair spiked and tousled. He draped the towel around his neck, held an end in each hand and gave her a half smile. "Better."

This was the most unkempt she'd ever seen him. It was rather endearing.

"You need a shower and dry clothes." She lit two candles, offered them to him. "Did you eat?"

"No. I just wanted to get home."

Thunder boomed overhead. Lightning flashed, then flashed again.

Tori shivered. "If you promise to hurry, I'll heat something up for you while you shower."

The offer earned her a full grin, the smile that tugged

at something deep in her. The grin along with the disheveled hair made him appear younger, more approachable.

"Best offer I've had all day." He raised a cereal bowl as if toasting her with the candle. "Be right back."

The house felt different with Garrett in residence. The storm still raged, but the darkness no longer oppressed. In front of the open refrigerator she surveyed her choices. She pulled out the leftover stew and a tube of prebaked biscuits and went to work.

"Smells good." Garrett came into the kitchen dressed in a sweatshirt and jeans.

"Almost ready." Tori closed the oven door and set the pan of biscuits on the stove top. "Take a seat at the table."

She placed the food in front of him and curled into a chair across the table to watch him eat. A companionable silence fell between them.

After a few minutes, she fought off a yawn and decided to give him a progress report. "The crews finished—"

He held up a hand to stop her. "Not tonight. I've had all the meetings I can handle today."

"It's good news," she tempted him.

He shook his head. "I don't care." He shoved in another bite of stew.

"Okay." Snatching a hot biscuit, she smeared it with butter and grape jelly. "Mmm," she moaned.

He froze with a biscuit halfway to his mouth. "None of that, either."

She frowned. "I can't have a biscuit?"

"You can't make those lovey-dovey noises."

She blinked at him. "What are you talking about?"

He pinned her with an intense stare. "Those little moans you make when you eat. I'm too tired to ward them off tonight."

"Oh." His comment gave her a lot to process. She hadn't realized she made lovey-dovey sounds when she ate. More important was the attraction he'd revealed with his admission. Sure there'd been a couple of kisses and the dance the other night, but his stoic professionalism discouraged any fraternization between them.

A policy she respected and agreed with. A policy she'd be smart to heed tonight.

Because of the party nature of what she did, it was important to be ever mindful of mixing pleasure with clients. With Garrett, she needed to take extra care.

He hid a lost soul behind his all-business facade.

For good reason. Abandoned by his mother, raised by an emotionally stunted father, later rejected by him. His fiancée left him over a career choice. Any one of these things was enough to damage a person's confidence. Add them together and it was no wonder he wanted to protect himself.

His vulnerability called to her.

But she couldn't heal his pain. She'd reached out to Shane, tried to fix their bruised friendship. But ultimately she couldn't give him what he needed. They'd been so close, and she'd failed. She still reeled from the loss she'd suffered so long ago.

No, she couldn't heal Garrett's pain. Only he could do that, either by forgiving the wounds of the past or by being strong enough to open himself to the possibilities of the future, of new relationships.

But tonight, none of that seemed to matter. They were two people holding off a storm raining havoc around them. Cocooned by the flicker of candlelight, they'd become reliant on each other, drawn together by the intimate circumstances.

She didn't need to touch his soul. His broad shoulders, those hard abs, were enough to get her through the night.

Holding his desire-darkened gaze, she deliberately lifted the other half of her biscuit and took a bite.

"Mmm," she moaned. A dollop of jelly fell on her finger. She made a sensual display of removing the sweetness from her skin with slow licks of her tongue.

An actual growl rumbled from his throat. "I only give one warning."

She wrapped her lips around her finger then slowly drew it out. "Are you done with your meal?"

"I'm finished." He stood and placed his bowl and the nearest candle on the counter. Then he came to her, passion burning in his eyes. He lifted her to him, claimed her mouth in a breath-stealing caress.

"But I'm still hungry." He swept everything else on the table aside with one swipe of his arm and laid her on the wooden surface. A biscuit flew through the air. The second candle almost toppled.

He didn't care. He buried his face in her neck, nibbling and kissing a trail to the tip of her chin. Her skin tingled with every little nip, her blood heated. He stopped for a kiss, a wild tangling of tongues, before beginning a downward descent.

OMG. She needed to halt him now, or they'd set the house on fire. Literally.

"Garrett." His name came out as more of a groan than a bid for attention. His fault. How was she supposed to think with his talented hands stroking over sensitive flesh? She tried again. "Garrett."

"Don't stop me." His teeth sank into the curve of her shoulder in sensual warning. "You chose this."

"I'm not." She arched into him, her blood humming from the pleasurable sting of his bite. "Bedroom," she said desperately.

"Here," he decreed and licked a path up her neck to the tender spot behind her ear. She shivered as need built in her.

"The candle will fall."

"Let it."

She laughed, moaned. "Your house."

"Mine," he agreed and stripped her sweater over her head.

She cradled his head, threading her fingers into the silky thickness of his hair to hold his mouth where she wanted it most. He gave her the attention she craved, laving her through the lace of her bra. The heat of his breath seared her skin, ignited her senses, sent her mind spinning.

Hunger for more of him had her tugging at his sweatshirt as she fought to get to his skin, all that yummy flesh stretched over hard muscles. "Mmm." Suddenly his mouth was on hers, cutting off the ardent whimper. His erotic penalty coaxed more lovey-dovey sounds from her throat, from her soul.

"Off." She dug her fingers into the thick fabric and yanked. "Now."

He stood, grabbed a handful of sweatshirt and pulled it over his head. In those few seconds the chill in the room wafted over her heated form. Losing his weight, his warmth revealed just how icy the room had grown. When he lowered to her, she planted her hands in the middle of his chest.

"It's freezing in here. And the table is hard." She cupped his cheek. "Can we please move to the bedroom? Mine is just across the hall."

He leaned his forehead on hers. "If it's comfort you want, mine is better."

"You win."

"Oh, I know." He helped her to her feet, tucked her under his arm and started out of the room.

"Wait." She tried to pull away to grab the candle at the end of the table.

"Oh, no you don't. Things I want have a way of slipping through my fingers. I'm not letting you go until I have you in my bed."

Her heart wrenched at his revealing comment. She looped her arms around his neck. "I'm not going anywhere," she promised. "Not until morning."

"That works for me."

Garrett let Tori get the candle, then took her hand and led her to his bed. Savage satisfaction roared through every cell at the sight of her golden hair flowing across his pillow in the soft glow of the candlelight.

He took the candle she carried and set it on the bedside table. He'd left another burning on his dresser across the room. The dimness allowed him to see her but wrapped them in intimacy.

Tori loved the sunshine and her lightly tanned skin blended with the soft beige of her lacy bra. Her lovely breasts rose and fell with each breath and her pulse raced under his fingers at her wrist, all signs of the desire in her molten gaze.

Beautiful.

He stood back, admiring the look of her in his bed. But need beat at him, poured through his blood like the liquid gold staring up at him, driving lust through every extremity. He craved the feel of her, longed to touch, to taste. Not any woman, but her.

He couldn't remember the last time he'd felt such all-consuming, primitive lust.

Holding her gaze, he reached for the button of her jeans. She lifted her hips, making it easy for him to remove her pants and thong. She sat up, giving him access to her bra clasp as her fingers went to work at his waistband.

"Let me." His hands shook slightly as he accomplished the task, but were steady when he lowered himself to her, pulling her in for a deep kiss. She tasted of honey and spice, intoxicating.

Her hands fisted in his hair and she arched into his embrace, a plea—no, a demand—for him to hurry. The small noises he found so irresistible whispered into his ear.

He gave into her insistent entreaty, stroking and soothing, nibbling and kissing every inch of her, and she matched him caress for caress, kneading, licking, sinking her fingers into his muscles.

"Garrett," she gasped his name, made it an endearment.

Her responsiveness torched his restraint and he took them higher, faster, reaching for the sky, touching the stars as fulfillment sent their senses spinning and their bodies shuddered harder than the house at the apex of the storm.

CHAPTER TEN

THERE WAS A MAN in Tori's bed. A warm, hard-muscled, naked man pressed snug against her back. She went from cozy and sleepy and—oh, yes—satisfied to panicked in 0.2 seconds.

OMG, the bed belonged to Garrett Black.

Okay, okay, she needed to calm down, to think beyond the roar of her pulse in her ears. Breathe, that's what she needed to do. She inhaled a slow, deep breath. And choked on her own air when the action rubbed her bare skin over the hair-roughened chest of the man behind her.

Big mistake. No more breathing.

She opened her eyes and looked directly at the shallow remains of a candle on the bedside table. She frowned and blinked. Then the events of the previous night came flooding back. The storm, the fear and loneliness, relief when Garrett arrived, heating stew and…dessert.

She swallowed back a moan. One minute she and Garrett had been chatting over leftovers, the flicker of candlelight adding to the intimate mood, the next they'd both lost their minds and the moment had gone beyond the boundaries of a professional relationship.

Lauren was going to kill her. Employee-client fraternization was much worse than taking her heels off at an event.

Tori had reasons of her own why last night should never have happened.

Unnerved by the storm and being caught in the dark in an unfamiliar house, she'd let the coziness in the kitchen go to her head. In an unexpected move he'd put business off-limits, which left her defenseless. She got swept away by the closeness of the moment and lowered her guard.

He'd sat across from her, relaxed and comfortable in sweatshirt and jeans, his hair disheveled from the rain and his recent shower. For such a strong, confident man, he'd looked…ruffled.

Sexy.

Vulnerable.

And entirely too approachable.

Everything after that took on a sensual haze: a tangled limbs, heated skin, breath-stealing, wonderful haze. She'd reached heights last night where she'd actually touched fireworks.

Her blood still hummed.

Behind her Garrett stirred, his hand burned a brand on her hip.

Tori froze, her heart pounding as she waited for him to wake, to speak, to regret what happened between them. And he would regret the night of passion. She knew how he felt about keeping the world at a distance. How fanatically he protected his heart.

He stirred again and rolled on to his back.

Sighing, she allowed herself to breathe again. After a few minutes, enough to figure he'd settled into sleep, she slowly began to inch away from the heat of his body. Immediately she missed the warmth and safety of being enveloped in his arms. Determinedly she pushed the illusion away.

Did she regret the passionate interlude?

Oh, yeah.

She liked her job, liked the challenge of it, the glamour, the satisfaction of keeping up with Garrett's fast-paced intelligence. By Arrangement still had several events to complete for the studio. She didn't want to put their reputation at risk because of a slip of judgment and a surge of hormones.

Especially when no chance of a future existed for her and Garrett. She'd experienced firsthand the pain and loss that came from loving someone emotionally injured, someone who lived in a perpetual cycle of angst. She'd sworn never to put herself in that situation again.

On her feet, she slipped into his shirt. No way was she taking the time to dress. Besides, there was no sign of her sweater, which meant it probably littered the floor of the kitchen.

She may never wear the sweater again. Too many memories.

Avoiding the sight of his large body sprawled under the sheets, she tiptoed about, gathering clothes, blushing when she found her lace thong buried under his black boxer briefs. Vivid memories of how the snug fabric clung to his muscular body assailed her. Swallowing back an urge to drool, she snatched up the thong.

She debated waking him to discuss the situation and how it affected their business relationship, but decided nothing could be gained by rushing the confrontation. Far better if time and distance separated them when they discussed the events of last night.

Thank God the work here was nearly finished. It was beyond time for her to return to her duplex. Hopefully she could pack and escape before she encountered Garrett.

Decision made, she headed for the door.

"Tori?"

She stilled, her hand wrapped around the knob as the husky voice reached her. Fingers flexing on the brass knob, she stared at the heavy oak door. "Yes."

Sleep thickened his next words. "It's best we forget this ever happened."

"Yes." Equal parts of relief and, surprisingly, disappointment rushed through her. "It's best forgotten."

With a sigh she quietly stepped outside and pulled the door closed behind her.

"Are you going to be seeing Ray tonight?" Tori asked to take her mind off Garrett and their mad night of passion.

If she stopped concentrating for two seconds, memories, regrets, wishes took her mind over in a flash. Little of it made sense, some was just irrational and none of it was productive. *Self-destructive* was the best word to describe her mental gymnastics. She just needed to stop.

She thought it would help them both to move beyond that night if she set him up with his next date. It hadn't. Not her, anyway.

Who knew how he was doing?

He hadn't talked to her since she'd left the house. She'd sent him the information about his date, which was for the opening reception of the film festival, through email. He'd simply responded he'd see her there. A none-too-subtle reminder for her to be available to rescue him if necessary.

She'd been looking forward to tonight. The reception was one of the few events she and Lauren were attending instead of working.

Now she had to spend the night watching Garrett with another woman. She accepted the two of them had no future together. Still, seeing him escorting someone else was not her idea of fun.

"He'll probably be there," Lauren answered her question about Ray. "But I told you there's nothing between us."

"No, you said what was between you was over. That it was just a flash in the pan." Tori watched her sister's profile as she drove. "I can't believe you did it in the laundry room with Mom and Dad in the house." Actually, she couldn't believe Lauren did it in the laundry room at all. She didn't normally do spontaneous.

Lauren flicked Tori a narrow-eyed glance. "You promised you'd never say anything to them."

"And I won't," Tori assured her. "That's not a conversation I want to have." But focusing on her sister's love life beat brooding on her own. "So you won't say hello?"

"Not unless we end up in the same group." From her tone, the likelihood seemed slim.

It appeared they were in the same boat tonight.

"Tell me about Garrett's date." Lauren changed the conversation.

Tori turned her gaze to the lights flashing by her window. She hadn't told Lauren about sleeping with Garrett and it ate at her. They were partners. Lauren had a right to know. More, they were sisters, twins. Tori couldn't know about the laundry room without being honest about the night of the storm.

"I slept with Garrett."

"What?" Lauren's head swung her way.

"Watch out!" Tori threw up a bracing hand as Lauren slammed on the brakes at a red light. "Sorry."

Lauren gave her a look, and when the light changed she pulled through the intersection and into a parking lot. She put the car in gear, turned off the ignition and faced Tori.

"Spill."

"It just happened." She tried for a careless shrug. "Like you and Ray."

"Try again. We have no open contracts with Ray."

"I know, okay." Tori stared at her hands to avoid the censure in her sister's expression. "It shouldn't have happened. I've been careful to keep things as professional as possible. But the storm…" Tori shook her head. "Don't worry, it won't happen again."

Lauren's warm grip settled over Tori's restless fingers. "Tell me about the storm."

Tori glanced over and swallowed hard when she saw it was her sister asking, not her partner. The words bubbled out of her then, about being caught in the dark and being spooked. How happy she was when Garrett got home and how sexy he looked all disheveled and ruffled. And oh, the way he looked at her, all hot and bothered.

"And?" Lauren prompted when she finished.

Tori hesitated for half a second. "And OMG, it was magical. I have seen the creative side of Garrett Black."

"Award worthy?" Lauren grinned.

Heat rushed to Tori's cheeks. "Oh, yeah."

"So why did you set him up with another date?"

She sighed. "Because he's a client, and emotionally constipated, and it would never work between us."

"Emotionally constipated?" Lauren about choked on the phrase. "Is that another way of calling him a shit?"

"It means he's blocked. He's been hurt so many times he protects his heart like it's made of gold." Tori bit her lower lip, already swollen from days of similar torture. "Oh, Lauren, sometimes I see the same look in Garrett's eyes I used to see in Shane's."

"God, Tori. Garrett has had a really tough year, but you can't possibly think he'd—"

"No, of course not," Tori quickly denied, not allowing Lauren to finish. The man had way too much ego to give up. But that didn't mean he was willing to live life to the fullest. "At least, I don't think so. But then, I never would have thought it of Shane, either."

"Shane was a boy, a selfish, immature child who felt the world owed him." Lauren didn't sugarcoat her opinion. "Garrett is a man who has suffered much and not only has he endured, he's a successful director and businessman."

"I know. Of course, I know." Lauren wasn't saying anything Tori hadn't told herself. "But he's blocked himself off, just as Shane withheld himself from me. No matter what I did I couldn't reach him. I can't go through that again."

Lauren squeezed her hand, asked softly, "Do you care for Garrett?"

"More than I should," Tori confessed. "Which makes it all the more imperative I put the brakes on now."

"So you never feel any vibe when you're with Garrett?" Lauren asked her. "Nothing to give you a clue that you belong together?"

Totally unprepared for the question, Tori blinked at her. "Like our matchmaking vibe? No. And I'm glad. It would be terrible to know we were meant for each other when he's so out of reach."

"Right." Lauren got them back on the road. "Do you want me to take Garrett duty tonight?"

Tori wished. "No. You may as well enjoy the party. I won't be able to keep from watching him anyway." She remembered Lauren's original question. "I went outside the industry for this date. Mari is a financial advisor. Stocks, retirement funds, that kind of thing. She's a brown-eyed brunette, striking rather than pretty."

"Good choice. He'll appreciate someone with brains."

"Some men preferred beauty to brains."

"Uh-huh."

Tori crossed her arms over her chest. "Just drive."

The film festival chose a rooftop ballroom in a beautiful old hotel on Sunset Boulevard for the opening reception. Garrett looked on the red carpet as a necessary evil. His strategy involved powering forward until a microphone got shoved in his face.

His date, Mari, carried herself well. Exotic brown eyes changed her average features from plain to interesting.

Her floor-length navy sheath dress clung to slim curves. When asked what she was wearing, she simply replied she'd picked it up at a boutique in Hollywood.

"And here we have Garrett Black, the new president of Obsidian Studios." A perky blonde from a prime-time entertainment show stepped into his path. He exchanged pleasantries. Then she asked, "What's it like being on the executive side of the industry? Does it mean you've given up directing?"

"I'm still evaluating my options," he responded vaguely, then added, "The studio is excited to celebrate its ninetieth anniversary at the film festival."

"Yes, the party is being held at The Old Manor House from the classic horror film," the woman gushed. "I have to say it's one of the events I'm most looking forward to."

"I'm glad to hear it. I hope to see you there."

"I wouldn't miss it. Thanks, Garrett Black." The blonde nodded to them and moved to her next victim.

Garrett mixed up his comments to include some of the premieres planned for the film festival but by far the most enthusiastic reaction was anticipation of the anniversary party. He had to hand it to Tori, she'd made the right call there.

As if her name magically conjured her, the crowd parted and there she stood. He was used to seeing her in black or jeans. Tonight she wore a short dress in holly berry-red. The dress clung and shimmered with every move she made. The bodice angled up to ring her neck, leaving her beautiful shoulders bare.

When she turned, he nearly choked on a sip of champagne. The back consisted of a single red strip from her neck to her waist. She'd bundled her long blond tresses into a loose bun on top of her head, leaving all her silky skin on display.

His fingers twitched with the need to touch.

She glowed bright as a flame and with her ready smile she brought light and warmth wherever she went. He felt it all the way across the crowded room.

"Garrett. Garrett?" A hand touched his arm and he glance down into Mari's slanted gaze.

"Did you want to mingle?" she asked.

"Yes, of course. Is there anyone in particular you'd like to meet?" He found there usually was.

She brightened. "Do you think Meryl Streep is here?"

How novel. It was usually George Clooney.

"Possibly, shall we see?" He offered her his arm and they made a turn around the room.

He tried, and failed, to keep his eyes off Tori. She drew him like an elf to Santa's workshop. She was a bright gift he longed to unwrap.

He'd been surprised to get her email informing him of his date for tonight. It just felt wrong. He'd even considered suggesting the two of them pretend to hook up to satisfy her need to please the starlets.

But once he thought about the situation, he realized it would be a mistake to let the feisty minx get any more entrenched in his life. He already had to deal with constant recollections of her passionate caring, of being wrapped in her arms. Any insecurity he felt about his leg vanished under her soft touch. She never flinched as she kissed each scar.

He still smelled her in his house, still heard the echo of her chatter.

Who knew he'd miss it?

Exactly why he needed to put her from his thoughts, why he needed to forget the memory of her sweet response. So the house felt empty. He could live with that. He couldn't live with losing anyone else. Except he'd never actually had anyone, had he? Mother, father, fiancée, they were all supposed to love you, but they'd all walked away from him.

He could only conclude he lacked whatever it took to attract love. Better to be alone than to continually be judged wanting.

He enjoyed talking to Mari. She had a sharp mind and a quick wit. He'd be happy to have her in his accounting department, but there was no spark. And that suited him just fine.

"Good evening, Garrett." Tori snuck up on him as he stood looking out at the spectacular view.

"Tori." He inclined his head. "You look lovely this evening."

"You, too. Where did you stash Mari?" She propped her hands on her curvy hips. "You didn't put her in a car home, did you?"

"No. I introduced her to my chief financial officer."

Her eyes widened. "You palmed her off on someone else?"

He lifted a dark eyebrow, a silent reprimand. "I left them talking. They really seemed to hit it off. Perhaps I have talent as a matchmaker."

She sent her eyes heavenward. "Oh, you're a hoot."

"Relax. I have no desire to be a marriage broker."

"You don't understand. It's not a matter of marriage but of soul mates."

"Come on." He mocked her. "We both know you and your sister dreamed up the matchmaking scheme to drum up business. If you introduce a couple, they're hardly likely to go to another event coordinator."

She paled. "That's not true. And it's a terrible thing to say."

"So you haven't handled any of the weddings?"

"Yes, but it wasn't some diabolical, preconceived plan like you're suggesting." He'd clearly insulted her. "We've matched up plenty of couples and got nothing out of it."

"Then why bother?" He wasn't being cynical. He could understand matchmaking as a good marketing plan. It was an effective gimmick. But as an altruistic act? That was beyond his comprehension.

"Why?" Her brow furrowed in bafflement. "How could we not? People search their whole lives for love. If we can help them find the special someone to grow old with, we feel it's our obligation to do so. If anything, it's complicated our work. As you can attest."

"So you do it out of the goodness of your hearts."

"Pretty much."

"And you don't care if they get married?" He would have taken her for a white-picket-fence gal.

She shifted, turning to look out the picture window. "How people choose to be together is their own business."

"That doesn't sound like a wedding planner," he pointed out.

"Just because I believe in marriage doesn't mean everyone does. Some people feel a marriage certificate is just a piece a paper. Some still get married, others don't. We assist the ones who do." She swung around, the action putting her between him and the window, mere inches away. Her chin went up and her hands landed on her hips. "Why the interrogation, Garrett? Are you thinking of getting married? Did you connect more with Mari than you let on? Because no matter how good I am at forgetting certain things ever happened, By Arrangement would have to respectfully decline planning your wedding."

"I'm not attracted to Mari, and I would never ask you to."

"Good."

Was it his imagination or did she relax a little? Her scent distracted him. She usually smelled of her cherry blossom lotion. Tonight he inhaled an intoxicating musk.

"So why all the questions?" she persisted.

"Just curious."

"About matchmaking and marriage?"

He understood her puzzlement. Truthfully, he was unsure what drove him. "I just made an offhand comment, you took it from there. Still, I'd like to know, what does marriage mean to you? Is it just a piece of paper?"

Her eyes delved into his, probably questioning his sanity. Finally she answered.

"No, when I get married, I hope it'll be forever. I want my vows to have meaning and value, and for my promises to be made before God because it matters."

She cocked her head. "Now I'm curious. You were engaged once. What does marriage mean to you?"

CHAPTER ELEVEN

GARRETT SCOWLED, TOOK a step back. Suddenly he'd had enough of this conversation. Tori's hand landed on his tux-covered arm, blocking his retreat.

"Oh, no, you don't. I answered all your questions."

What the hell? "I thought it meant committing ourselves to each other, being there through the tough times. I was wrong. I should have known better. That was one lesson I should have learned from good old Dad."

"So you gave up on relationships. But not sex."

His eyebrow shot up. She should know the answer to that. "I don't have to be in a relationship to have sex."

Her eyes flashed. Oh, yeah, she remembered. She shook her finger at him. "I'm talking about bad sex. You don't give on sex because of a bad experience. You shouldn't give up on love, either."

He stared at her. "Are you saying the sex was bad for you?"

"No." Shock crossed her delicate features. "It was…" He saw the exact moment when her mind caught up with her emotions. "Adequate."

Ouch. But he was too gratified by her reaction to let her attempt at retaliation get to him. He bent over her ear, whispered, "Liar."

She pushed him back with a finger in the center of his chest. "You're missing the point."

He wrapped his hand around hers, swept his thumb over the skin at her wrist. So soft.

"The thing about bad sex is once it's over, you're done and gone. A bad relationship stays with you forever."

As if the admission jarred a nerve, something shifted in him. Feeling exposed, he lifted her hand to his mouth and kissed her palm. "Good night, Tori."

"W-wait." She cleared her throat. "What about our arrangement?"

He lifted one shoulder, let it drop in a gesture of unconcern. "Enjoy your evening. I think I'm safe with Mari. Now if you'll excuse me, there's Meryl Streep. I promised Mari an introduction."

Tori watched his broad shoulders disappear in the crowd. She rubbed a spot over her heart. What an odd conversation. And how dare he blame her? He'd been the one with all the questions.

Was it her fault he didn't care to have the tables turned on him? She thought for a moment he might really open up to her. Maybe he had. *A bad relationship stays with you forever.* Did that mean he still had feelings for his former fiancée? That wasn't the impression she'd gotten before tonight.

And she didn't like the thought of it now. One thing tonight revealed, she was in worse trouble than she wanted to admit. As of now, Garrett duty went to Lauren.

Because watching him walk away to be with another woman broke her heart more than a little.

Four days and three events later Tori did a final walk-through of The Old Manor House. Outside the house maintained the classic appearance the guests would expect to see; inside the beauty and warmth of the Christmas holiday invited the guests to come in and celebrate the season and Obsidian Studios' ninetieth anniversary.

When she walked through the foyer, she came across Garrett staring at the largest tree they'd bought together. It stood in the middle of the entry hall, a sentinel of the event.

"What do you think?" The decorations had just been completed this afternoon. She'd sweated the timing but she'd special ordered the ornaments and they hadn't arrived until this morning. It turned out better than she hoped.

"I have no words," Garrett said. "How did you do this?"

"Anything is available for a price. Time was our biggest factor, but it worked out." Decorated in silver bows, red crystal holly berries and gold statues, the tree sparkled from every direction. Each mini Academy Award–shaped statue bore the name and date of an award-winning movie, actor, director and so forth earned by Obsidian Studios films over the past ninety years.

"It's stunning."

He was pretty stunning himself in an Armani tuxedo. "There are actually more statues than the tree could hold. The rest are bunched in displays throughout the party area."

He stepped close. "I've been here through the whole process and I'm still amazed with what you've done."

"It's what we do," she said simply.

"No. This is all you." He tugged softly on the end of her sleek ponytail. "You went beyond the call of duty. Thank you."

"All part of the service." She played it cool. "Tomorrow is the end of the film festival. This is our last event together. I want to say it's been interesting working with you."

"Interesting?"

Surprisingly they'd managed to put personal matters aside the past few days and work very well together. Obsidian's events were the talk of the festival along with Ray's film and an independent production that was getting lots of good press. After tonight's party, no one would talk about the film festival without mentioning Obsidian Studios.

"How would you describe it?" she wondered.

"Parts of it were quite pleasurable."

Of course he had to go there. She'd spent the past four days pushing every hint of their sensuous interlude from her mind. Keeping up a professional facade had been the only way to see him daily and retain her sanity.

"We agreed to forget those parts."

"I haven't been as successful at forgetting as I'd like." His gaze ran over her, approval in the silver depths. "You look lovely tonight."

She wore a black cocktail dress with a V-neck, off-the-shoulder sleeves and a flowing skirt that showcased her legs. An ornate clip adorned a sleek side ponytail. The outfit was dressier than her usual garb when working, but tonight she considered herself a hostess.

"You set the rules, Garrett," she reminded him. "You can't change them now."

"But you're a rule breaker." He ran a finger down her cheek. "Don't think I've forgotten."

She caught his hand, pulled it down. "Not when it comes to my heart."

"The first car has arrived." The warning came through her headset from the valet station.

"Your first guest is here." She squeezed his hand and released it. "Have fun tonight. We'll take care of everything."

Garrett stood on the terrace with the film festival officials talking about the overall success of the festival when Ray joined the group.

"Well done," Ray addressed the officials. "This festival is the best I've been to this year. And Garrett Black, here,

is the man of the hour." Ray clapped Garrett on the back.
"You put Obsidian Studios in the hot spot."

"He did indeed," Martin, a portly gentleman, agreed.
"We were just talking about the high energy of the festival
this year, not least of which is due to Obsidian's events.
Both premieres got a lot of buzz, but the open house is the
talk of the festival."

Still stunning in her late sixties, the grand dame of the
festival, Estelle, hooked her arm through Garrett's. "The
Art Deco decor made you feel as if you were walking
back in history to Old Hollywood. Dressing the waitstaff
in fashions of the era was brilliant."

"My event coordinators are By Arrangement. They've
done an outstanding job."

"Truly spectacular." Estelle waved her hand to encom-
pass the terrace. "The decorations are lovely, well-placed
and tasteful, but it's also comfortable and welcoming. I
especially like the conversational area around the fire pit
and the fact there are lap blankets if anyone gets chilled.
Martin, make a note of By Arrangement."

"Of course. Garrett, you'll send me their information?"

"It would be my pleasure." Moving them along, Garrett suggested, "Estelle, why don't you try out the fire pit."

"I believe I will." She kissed Garrett's cheek and the
pair wandered off.

"Thanks for coming tonight and agreeing to do the anniversary toast." Garrett led Ray inside to a pub table in
the corner of the parlor.

"I'm happy to do it. Some of my best work has been
with Obsidian."

"I heard your film got some good quotes."

"Yeah. We're getting some award buzz. Nothing re-
sembling Obsidian, though. Congratulations, bro, you're
already making your mark on the company." Ray took
a sip of beer. "I was angry when you closed my set and

messed with my schedule, but it was a smart move. The studio's reputation was suffering, but it's already turning around." He tapped his beer bottle against Garrett's Champagne glass. "I predict good things for Obsidian in the coming years."

"I'll drink to that." Garrett lifted his glass to his lips.

"Those two did a hell of a job." Ray nodded his head toward the hall where Tori and Lauren stood together surveying the scene.

"The Dynamic Duo," Garrett agreed. He caught the way his buddy eyed the women and his back went up. He turned a narrowed gaze on his friend, for some odd reason feeling proprietorial about the twins. "I saw the tabloid with you and Lauren. What's going on there?"

Ray lifted a sandy-colored brow. "What's your interest?"

"I've worked closely with the girls." He put the weight of his concern in his voice. "I'd hate to see either of them hurt."

Ray laughed. "Dude, you sound like their big brother."

"I'm serious, Ray."

"No need to worry about me and Lauren." Ray held up a pacifying hand. "It was a few moments out of time, not to be repeated. Seriously, dude, instead of me, you should look to yourself."

Garrett stilled. "There's nothing between me and Tori."

"I'm a director, Garrett. I have a trained eye. There's more sexual tension between the two of you than Brad and Angelina."

"You're imagining things," Garrett denied.

"If that's true, you need to stop gazing at her as if she's the last lollipop." Ray stepped between Garrett and Tori, breaking his line of sight. "Because she looks at you like most women covet chocolate, and if you're going to close her out the way you do most people, she will get hurt."

"Do you have a sudden candy fetish?" Garrett frowned his annoyance. "Who's sounding like their brother now?"

"You brought it up," Ray pointed out. He swung around so they both faced the twins. "I'm fond of them, too, but you saw their family. They have to believe in love, marriage and happily ever after, which puts them firmly out of our reach."

Garrett said nothing. Because there was no arguing with the truth.

"Woo-hoo!" Tori kicked her shoes off and wrapped her sister in a big hug. "The last guest is gone. We did it. The Obsidian contract is done. Once the cleaning is over, of course." Maria and her crew would be here first thing in the morning. The food service had already packed up and left.

Lauren gave her a squeeze. "Yep, and people are going to be talking about this party for years. You did a great job."

"We did a great job. We're a team."

Lauren framed Tori's face. "No, this one goes to you. It was your genius idea. You pushed Garrett. You put the time into the house and decorations. The victory on this party is yours. Congratulations."

"This party was just the crowning glory. Everyone was talking about Obsidian's events tonight. We were a hit."

"On that we agree." Lauren walked to the table and poured them each a glass of champagne. "To By Arrangement."

Tori clicked classes. "Only one more party, then we're off until New Year's Eve. I'm ready for a holiday."

"Amen." Lauren clinked glasses again.

Tori dropped into a chair. She propped her head on her hand, sighed deeply, then peeked at her sister. "Well, except for planning another date for Garrett. You're really okay with handling that?"

"About that." Lauren slid into the seat across from Tori. "We're off the hook."

"What do you mean?" Exhaustion must be catching up with her because that didn't make sense.

"I saw Jenna and Cindy during the party. We got to talking and get this, they decided that having closed sets wasn't such a bad thing."

"You're kidding."

"Nope. It turns out they can focus on their roles and concentrate better when they don't have loved ones on set distracting them."

"Hmm. Who knew?" Tori rolled her eyes. Now they saw the wisdom of Garrett's rules, after she'd turned cartwheels to meet their matchmaking demands. And turned her heart inside out.

"I know." Lauren covered her hand. "But at least we don't have to continue with it. Shall we tell Garrett?"

"He drove the film festival officials back to their hotel. I lent him the SUV."

"Why didn't he just call them a cab?"

"Estelle was insistent."

"Gotcha." Lauren smothered a yawn. "I'm beat. Do you want me to drop you off? We can pick up the SUV tomorrow."

Tori was tempted. The Lord knew it had been a long week. "I'll wait. I want to do a last sweep through."

"I'll go with you."

"No, you go ahead. It'll only take a few minutes, and then I'll put my feet up and wait for Garrett." She walked Lauren to the door, watched her take off and then she locked the door and grabbed a trash bag.

She started on the terrace, brought in the lap blankets and turned off the lights. She found a diamond earring in the upstairs bathroom—someone would be calling about that—and a shawl pooled behind a poinsettia on the stairs.

The items went next to her purse on the coffee table. She'd see if Garrett wanted the studio to take charge of them or for By Arrangement to hold on to them.

She fought off a yawn. Garrett should be along anytime. Anytime...

Garrett stepped in the back door and made his way through the house in search of Tori. He saw some cleanup had yet to be done, but Tori told him a crew would be there in the morning. He hoped she wasn't trying to do anything more tonight. Sometimes he thought of her as an energized bunny, all go, go, go.

The Lord knew she lived life to the beat of her own drum. A beat that used to drive him crazy, but with the last of their events wrapped, he had to admit—if only to himself—he might miss her just a little. The characteristics he originally found irritating, her cheerful chatter, her wry humor, had grown on him. He'd always respected her intelligence and the way she challenged him.

Which all meant it was a good thing their contract was at an end. Ray thought Garrett had the power to hurt Tori, but what he didn't realize was Tori had the power to decimate Garrett. He didn't have it in him to be rejected again. Better to go through life lonely than shattered.

He walked into the parlor and found her asleep on the couch. He half smiled. So much for go, go, go. No surprise really. She arrived just after seven that morning, worked her shapely butt off all day and had juggled both the front and back of the house during the party. All on top of a very hectic week.

She looked lovely in the soft glow of the fire. Her golden hair picked up the flickering light, bringing it to life. Thick lashes fanned her cheeks, the creamy skin almost translucent in the dimness. The movement of her chest drew his gaze. Her breasts lifted and fell with each breath she took.

He remembered the taste of her, the softness, the perfection of her sensual responsiveness. But he pushed all that from his mind. Time for her to go.

Except he hated to wake her after such a long day. She'd done so much for him. Tonight's party wouldn't have been as successful at any other location. Successful, yes, but not special. She'd pushed for The Old Manor House, turned her life upside down to get it ready and delivered on a unique experience for every attendee.

The awards tree drew everyone's attention, shouting Obsidian's accomplishments without saying a single word. It was brilliant and creative, a gift he'd never forget.

"Tori," he said softly. She sighed but didn't move. "Tori," he spoke her name louder. Her keys jingled in his hand as he leaned over her.

"Hmm." She shifted, repositioning her shoulders, but she didn't awaken.

Enough. She'd slept here before; he'd just tuck her into bed and let her sleep.

He swept her up in his arms, inhaled her sweet scent. It only took a moment to reach the study, but of course the bed was in sofa mode. He should have thought to check before moving her. No problem. He'd just put her in his bed and sleep here himself.

He eyed the stairs. He'd experienced some aching with the recent damp weather. He worried briefly that it might give him trouble with Tori's extra weight. Being careful, he made it to the top without incident. Triumph trumpeted through him. The personal accomplishment proved he was still a man, capable of taking care of his woman in her weakest moment. *His woman?* Of course he meant *a woman.*

In his room he shouldered the light on, made his way to the bed and, grabbing the edge of the spread, pulled it back. He carefully laid Tori on the crisp white sheets. Before standing, he released her hair from the jeweled clip, letting the lush tresses loose to flow over his pillow. He set the clip on the night table and stepped back.

Never had he seen anything more beautiful, sleeping beauty in his bed.

He reached to remove her shoes, but, of course, they were already gone, her pretty, pink-tipped feet were bare against the bedding. He fondly shook his head. The woman was forever kicking off her shoes.

Okay, time to go when he started thinking a woman's feet were sexy. He grasped the spread, only he couldn't bring himself to pull it over her.

No. That wasn't the problem. He didn't want to leave her. And why should he? They'd shared a bed once; they could do so again. He dropped the covers over her. Then he stepped back and reached for his tie.

CHAPTER TWELVE

TORI WOKE TO an odd sense of déjà vu. A man was in her bed. Only this time there was no doubt in her mind of whom. Garrett. She clung to him like ivy wrapped around a trellis, her head on his chest, arm over his waist, legs entwined. His body cushioned hers, while his heat warmed her, inside and out.

The fuzziness came from how she got there.

The last thing she remembered was waiting for Garrett to get home last night. She must have fallen asleep in front of the fire. Which didn't actually explain how she ended up in his bed.

She sighed, not really caring how she got there. It felt too good to be snuggled up to him. Her mind screamed at her to peel away, to make a stealthy exit, just like last time. But she hadn't escaped unscathed. And this time she had no pleasure to offset the upset.

So she shut her mind to sense. Instead she gave in to her senses and turned her head to press her lips to the hard plains of his chest. In the pale light of dawn she drew lazy patterns in the dusting of hair on his pecs as she slowly kissed a path up his side. Lifting her head, she lightly nipped the ball of his shoulder and met pale gray eyes searing her through half-lowered lids.

"Good morning." The words came out in a husky purr.

"A most excellent morning." A bit of gravel made his early morning voice a sexy rumble.

She ran a finger down his shadowed jaw. "Did you take advantage of me last night?"

"I wanted to—" he bit the tip of her finger "—but I was a gentleman."

"Good. I wouldn't have wanted to miss anything."

"Hmm." He rolled so she was under him. "I find it's better when both parties participate."

"Mmm." She savored his weight pushing her into the mattress. Nothing quite equaled the sense of security and excitement that came with being wrapped in the arms of a strong man. She looped her arms around his neck, threaded her fingers in his thick hair, loving the softness against her skin. "It does add to the experience."

He buried his mouth in the curve of her neck, licked the spot behind her ear that made her body shudder with want.

"I need to brush my teeth." It was the first sensible thought in her head since she woke up. Maybe it would spark more, and she'd find the resolve to stop this before it went too far.

"Me, too." His breath feathered over skin as he kissed a path down her neck to the edge of her dress.

Her dress. Now she thought of it, she felt the skirt bounced around her thighs. How sweet of him. He could have stripped her or even left her in her underwear, they had been lovers after all. Instead he allowed her the modesty of her dress. How chivalrous.

But not something he chose for himself, she discovered as she ran her hands down the length of his back to the treasure of his tight derriere. She savored the feel of skin and muscles on the return journey.

"And a shower." An imperative, now that she knew she'd slept in her clothes.

"Good idea." He kissed her softly on the lips and slipped from the bed to sweep her into his arms.

"Garrett," she gasped, "I'm too heavy."

"Hardly." He walked into the bathroom. "How do you think I got you upstairs?"

"Oh, my Lord, I didn't thing about it. You shouldn't have. What about your leg?"

"It's fine." He dismissed her concern and set her down. He opened a drawer and handed her a new toothbrush. Then he took a black shaving bag from a cabinet and went to the door. The look he shot her made her toes curl against the cool tile. "I'm going to use the other bathroom. You have five minutes."

Tori lost thirty seconds of her allotted time peeking around the door, admiring his magnificent backside as he left the room. Then she hopped to, taking care of business before he returned. All too soon a knock sounded at the door.

"Come in." She struck a sultry pose, but when the door began to open she felt foolish and quickly dropped it so she stood one bare foot over the other. Her hair fell free over bare shoulders and she clasped a towel around her with one hand. With the other she twirled a piece of hair around her finger.

He stepped inside, his eyes darkening as he stalked her. Up close he framed her face in warm hands and lifted her face for kiss after kiss. He tasted of man and temptation.

She lost her hold on the towel to grip his shoulders, her body melded to his, skin to skin, curves to plains, lip to lip. Blood surged through her veins, spreading heat to every part of her. Anticipation sent butterflies fluttering.

He pulled back. Breathing hard, he rested his forehead against hers.

"You are so beautiful."

Eyes closed, she smiled. "When you look at me, I feel beautiful."

"I was afraid you'd come to your senses."

"Seriously? I was naked except for a towel."

He traced her jaw. "I meant while I was gone."

"No." Suddenly uncertain, she struggled to engage her mind through the fog of lust. "I should have just left, huh? It would have been the sensible thing to do." She bent and gathered up the towel.

"Sensible is overrated." He pulled her against him, reigniting her passion with a wild kiss. He lifted his head without releasing her and catching the edge of the door, he swung it closed. "You'll feel better after you shower."

Wrapped in a damp towel Tori used Garrett's hair dryer on her hair. Satisfaction lifted the corners of her mouth and hummed lightly through her body. She viewed Garrett from the corner of her eyes.

He leaned against the counter, arms crossed over his chest, watching her. A towel was draped low around his hips. Catching her scrutiny, he lifted one dark eyebrow.

She turned off the dryer. "You should dress," she urged, sweeping her hair into a knot and securing it with the jeweled clip. "The cleaning crew will be here soon."

"I like watching you."

She liked watching him, too, liked having his eyes on her. But as the buzz of his loving faded, common sense invaded. The wonder of being with him confirmed her worst fear. She loved him. But she could never be with him. He rejected love, preferred to live an isolated existence.

She needed people, family, a commitment that included open communication.

"I have to go." She edged past him into the bedroom, clutching her clothes to her chest.

He followed. "Why don't we give this a try?"

She stilled, blew at a loose piece of hair. Was he really suggesting a relationship? "Define *this*."

"Us. As lovers." He tucked the bothersome hair behind her ear. "It would have been awkward while By Arrangement was under contract, but the events are over now."

"True, but we hope the studio will want to rehire us for future events. If things end badly between us, that's not likely to happen." And his belief that isolation equaled safety guaranteed a bad ending.

"I can separate work and play."

She had no doubt. He'd been doing it for years. "Yeah, well, I'm not that sophisticated. You don't do relationships and, as good as this was, a random series of booty calls doesn't sound appealing."

He crowded her, leaned close to whisper in her ear. "I can change your mind. Let's go to breakfast, talk about it."

"I don't think that's a good idea." No, it was a very bad idea. She imagined he could all too easily change her mind. Just standing over her smelling of man and soap, he tempted her.

"Why not?"

"Because I'm already too emotionally involved for either of our comfort." No reason not to be honest. Nothing would get through to him faster. Her heart picked up speed, dread filling her as she contemplated leaving him.

And it did bring him to a stop. Hands on hips, he considered her.

She expected him to send her on her way, hoped for a gracious departure and the chance of a cordial future.

"Who is Shane?" he asked.

She blinked at him. That she hadn't expected. "What? Where did you hear the name?"

"From you. The night of the storm. You said his name just before you provoked me into making love to you."

"Really?" She didn't remember saying it, but she had

been thinking of Shane as she often did around Garrett. "He's not important." She backed toward the door. "A friend from high school."

"He must be important for you to mention him." Garrett advanced on her.

"Why do you care?" she wondered. She waved at the bed. "This is as far as we go. We have no future. There's no need to delve into our histories."

"Says the woman who searched for me online." He caught her hand, drew her to the bed to sit. "Tell me."

"It was a long time ago." Wanting space between them, she sat sideways, with her legs half off the bed. "I don't like to talk about it."

"If it's not important, why are you upset?"

"I'm not." She secured her towel. Really, she needed to get dressed. "It's ancient history."

"Not so ancient if you still think of him."

"I don't usually. Not for a long time, anyway."

"Then why now?" He pulled her foot into his lap, gently massaged the sole. "What does Shane have to do with us?"

There was that word again. *Us.* With all her heart she wished it were true, wished she could believe in it, in them. And for the first time she felt some of Shane's pain. She couldn't be what he wanted, couldn't feel what wasn't there. Just as Garrett couldn't give her the love and affection he'd cut from his life so long ago.

"Nothing. Everything." His touch, the muscle melting massage, vanquished her resistance. Maybe if she told him, he'd find his way back someday. "Shane lived across the street. We grew up together. Next to Lauren, he was my best friend. We really got close in middle school when his parents went through a divorce. He didn't like change and that was the mother of all changes. He hated having to split his time between his parents' houses. He told me I was the only sane thing in his life."

"Divorce is hard on kids. Most of us survive."

"Shane didn't. He committed suicide."

His fingers stilled and he raised his gaze to hers. She saw concern and compassion, all for her. "I'm sorry."

She knew in that moment he'd never take his own life. She'd always suspected his strength and self-discipline made it unlikely, but the way he focused his sympathy on her and away from Shane revealed his disdain for the act.

"His mother moved our sophomore year of high school and he had to change schools. He hated her for that. He was so upset and negative it was hard to be around him. His dad stopped trying. Shane felt rejected and betrayed by everyone.

"It was such a difficult time. He wanted to spend time with me and I wanted to help, but he wouldn't talk to me, he wouldn't open up. My mom said I helped just by being there for him. And I get that, but it's frustrating to be shut out. I felt helpless."

"The only place he felt safe was with you," he guessed.

"Pretty much. We talked every day but between different schools and work it seemed we saw less and less of each other. Then he learned I was dating a guy in my class. I didn't consciously keep it from him, but he could be jealous of me spending time with my own family so I just didn't mention it."

Those months had been the worst of her life, even more than after Shane passed. Seeing her friend suffering, not knowing what was in his head made her sad. And angry. Which was the reason she went out with the jock to begin with. It was so hard spending time with Shane, who was in turns sullen and withdrawn, that a carefree date seemed like heaven.

It took her a long time after Shane's passing to get over the guilt of that. She hadn't dated again until college.

"Did he hurt you?"

Again Garrett's concern was for her. She'd never heard his voice so hard, and she'd been the victim of its cutting edge a time or two.

"Not physically. He went ballistic. He loved me and we were meant to be together. He accused me of leading him on, of lying to him. I was a slut and I betrayed him. Just like everyone betrayed him. Nobody cared about him. Nobody understood him." Even after all this time, his accusations and contempt still hurt.

"I tried to explain I did love him, but as a brother, that I would always be his friend. But he wouldn't listen, not that day, and not in the weeks to follow. I tried to reach him. I left messages. I went to his house. His mom said he completely retreated into himself and he wasn't talking to her, either."

"And then he took his own life." Garrett said it for her, as if he understood how difficult it was for her to say.

"Yes. I did talk to him one last time. He sounded so despondent. I repeated what I'd said before, told him I missed him. He said he missed me, too, but it would be too hard to be around me knowing I didn't care for him the same way he cared about me. Two days later his mom called to tell me. He left a note saying he'd love me forever."

"Bastard." Surging to his feet, Garrett paced away.

"Garrett!"

"Sorry." He barked out the word, yet clearly felt no remorse. He went to his dresser, pulled out jeans and a T-shirt. "But he sounds like a self-absorbed punk who couldn't hack the reality of life and blamed you for his shortcomings while he took the easy way out." He dropped his towel and yanked the clothes on.

"Why are you so mad?"

"Because he hurt you and because you obviously associate me with this guy, and not in a good way."

Of course he caught the similarities and the significance of the story. "This is why I didn't want to have this conversation."

"You don't know me at all if you think I'd commit suicide."

"I don't believe you would, no. I haven't honestly thought so at any point. But did the notion occur to me, yes." She stood, hugged her dress to her chest. "Suicide is ugly. It's not something you just forget. I'm sorry if it offends you."

He stared at her with stark eyes, then turned away and raked his hands through his hair. "I'm not that weak."

"I know." Tired of clutching the towel, needing to be ready to leave when this grim discussion ended, she dropped the towel and quickly dressed. Stupidly a blush heated her cheeks when he spun and caught her in her underwear. Ignoring the irrational reaction, she pulled her dress over her head.

"If you didn't fear I'd kill myself—" he gritted through clenched teeth "—what's the deal?"

"I've seen the same look in your eyes as Shane used to get. A raw vulnerability immediately eclipsed by a chilling disconnect." Avoiding the accusation in his eyes, she tugged her skirt into place over her hips. "I understand it's a protective mechanism, cut off the need before it can hurt you."

"So Shane and I learned the same lesson. When life kicks you in the balls, you find a way to survive."

"Commendable." And so very sad. She made a move toward him, but he jerked back. She stopped, cleared the sudden lump from her throat. "But the problem with shutting out emotion is you close yourself off from any chance of getting past the hurt, of finding the happiness you secretly long for."

"Psychobabble," he dismissed. "I've heard it before. I don't need to hear it again."

"And that's why we can't have a bit of fun." She shrugged her right shoulder, trying for uncaring, though her heart was breaking. "You're dark and withdrawn, happy to bury your emotions and deny your loneliness.

"I need light and joy in my life. I like people and sharing my triumphs and struggles. You won't take a risk for love, and I'd risk everything." A glance around for her shoes and purse resulted in nothing. They must be in the parlor. "But I can't divorce my body and emotions, and I wouldn't want to. Even in a fling I can't be with someone who closes me out. I won't go through the pain of sitting on the sidelines again."

She blinked back tears, swallowed the lump in her throat.

"I don't believe you'll take your own life, but I never conceived of Shane doing so, either. As long as you bury your pain instead of dealing with it, the risk is there." Her heart pounded in her chest, it felt as if a fist were squeezing the organ, slowly crushing it. She backed to the door. No more. She had to end this. "Losing him nearly broke me. If I lost you, it would destroy me."

CHAPTER THIRTEEN

"I MADE YOU a cup of jasmine tea." Lauren came into the room carrying a tray with two mugs.

"Thanks." Tori sat up on the beige ultrasuede couch and pulled another tissue from the box on the huge ottoman Lauren used as a coffee table. Tori mopped her cheeks while Lauren set the tray down. Mom always served jasmine tea when they were upset. The smell comforted her, making her wish Mom were here.

Tori would have left for Palm Springs today if they didn't have an event Monday night.

"Are you sure Garrett has no feelings for you?" Lauren sipped her tea. "The fact he wanted to have a fling tells me there's something there."

Tori sent her an arch glance. "Good sex."

Lauren returned the look.

"Really good sex." Tori sighed and stared into her mug. "Fantastic, blow-your-mind good sex."

"Which makes me ask again, are you sure there's nothing more there? In my experience the more involved my heart the better the sex."

"It doesn't matter, because even if he felt something, he'd never admit it. Not to me, probably not to himself."

"I've seen the way he looks at you," Lauren said. "He's not indifferent. Ray noticed it, too."

"I don't deny the chemistry. I'm ashamed to say my

first reaction when he suggested being lovers was excitement. I was so tempted just to go with the moment and jump into his arms."

"Why didn't you?" Lauren asked softly. "You love him. There's no shame in wanting to be with him. If you went into the affair with your eyes open, maybe you could make it work."

Tori lifted teary eyes to her sister. "I can't be in someone's life and not be a part of it. Can you see me respecting those boundaries?"

"Considering you ask complete strangers personal questions, I suppose not."

"We'd both be miserable."

And Lauren was usually the first one to point that out. She hadn't been as close to Shane as Tori, but they'd been friends. Lauren had been the one to help Tori pick up the pieces of her life.

"I'm surprised you're in favor of it." A just-lovers relationship wouldn't offend Lauren, but the impetuosity of it would.

"Yes, well. I saw—" Lauren leaned forward to adjust her mug on the tea tray. "I mean, this is the first time I've seen you so gaga over someone. I would hate to see you lose out on something special."

More tears welled. Tori leaned her head on her twin's shoulder. "That's so sweet."

"So what are you going to do?"

"Move on." She willed the tears away. "Get through the holidays, then bury myself in work."

Lauren laid her head on top of Tori's. "Sounds like a plan."

"I can't talk to him again, Lauren. Will you handle the rest of the communications with Obsidian?"

"Of course."

"I sent a picture of the diamond earring to your email and put the original in the lockbox at the office."

Yes, focusing on work helped.

"I'll take care of it." Lauren took Tori's mug and set it on the tray. "Now, if I know you, you still have some Christmas shopping to do. How about some shopping therapy?"

A deep and familiar love welled in her shattered heart. "Now there's a plan."

"Mr. Black." Garrett's secretary hovered in his doorway. "Will we be getting off early tomorrow? Some of the others were wondering. It would be nice if I could put out an email."

He closed his eyes. Ah, damn. How had he forgotten Christmas? He should have arranged for gifts for the office staff. No doubt she would have reminded him except he'd been out of the office most of last week. He couldn't pass the chore off to her at this late date.

Tossing down his pen, he asked, "How many support staff do we have on this floor?"

"Eight, including myself."

"Right." The offices would be closed Wednesday through Friday for the holiday. The phones had barely rung. No reason to keep the support staff hanging around. "The staff can leave at one tomorrow."

"Thank you, Mr. Black. Have a nice evening."

He nodded and she left. Great, now he had to go shopping. He could let it go, but that just felt petty. His first thought was to call Tori and ask her advice. And that just pissed him off. He didn't need her to save him.

He didn't need to be saved at all. He wasn't about to off himself.

At his lowest point he may have wondered why he bothered, but his response had been to reach deeper, try harder. He never contemplated giving up.

TERESA CARPENTER   175

The insult injured him to the depths of his soul.

How could she think him that weak?

Unable to concentrate on work, he closed up and headed out. Maybe he'd do better at gift shopping. The fact Tori interfered with his work irritated him all over again. Nothing outside the physical demands of recovery and therapy had ever had the power to distract him from his career be it director or executive.

He restrained the urge to put the Maserati through its paces on the surface streets. Later, after he finished his shopping, he'd take to the freeway and open it up. Perhaps he'd drive to his place in Santa Barbara. His leg was much better. He could manage the daily trip. There was no longer a need to stay so close to the studio.

His decision had nothing to do with the fact the old place was now haunted with Tori's ghost. Wherever he went in the house, memories of her assailed him.

She had a nerve accusing him of being closed off. He savagely shifted gears. Hell and damnation. He'd shared more with her than he had with his fiancée.

Which might explain why his fiancée found it so easy to walk away.

He flinched at the traitorous thought, blamed Tori for it, as well.

Pulling into the parking garage for the Hollywood and Highland mall, he avoided the valet service—he needed no additional reminders of the blasted woman—found a parking spot and stepped out of the elevator to a view of the Hollywood sign.

His momentum petered out at that point. He pulled out his phone and called Ray. When his friend answered, he explained his dilemma. "Any suggestions for gifts?"

"You're asking me?" Ray laughed. "Except for my grandmother and aunt, I haven't bought a woman a gift in years. My assistant handles all that."

"What's his number?"

"Forget it. He's out of the country. Why don't you call Tori?" Ray suggested. "She'll know the perfect thing."

"Tori's out of the picture." The words cut deeper than Garrett expected.

Ray didn't answer for a moment. "Your choice or hers?"

"Our contract was at an end," Garrett reminded him. "What makes you think there was any choice involved?"

"Your tone, for one thing." Ray's rueful response was a testament to how well he knew Garrett. "And Tori genuinely enjoys helping people. She wouldn't need to be under contract to answer your question."

"Her choice," Garrett confessed. "I proposed an affair. She wasn't interested. End of story."

"You mean you offered to be her lover and she refused your no strings, no emotion relationship. I'm not surprised. I told you she wasn't the type."

"Well that's all I have to offer," Garrett stated, pushing down the panic that rose up when he probed at the guards he held so firmly in place. Tori was right about one thing, he was dark and unfeeling, too damaged to risk the light. Loneliness was the price he paid for peace of mind.

"If you have no gift ideas for me, I've got to go." Garrett rubbed a hand over the back of his neck.

"Hey," Ray said before Garrett could disconnect.

"Yeah?"

"For what it's worth, I think you'd be safe with her."

Garrett didn't know what to say, so he said nothing. Ray got it.

"Merry Christmas, buddy." The call ended with a soft chime.

Bastard. He said that to mess with Garrett's head, worse, to mess with his heart.

He started walking, window-shopping, except he saw little. His mind replayed every memory of his time with

Tori, kind of like a near death experience, from the time she tripped barefoot down Ray's front steps to leave her toe prints in his car, to the professional who challenged him in his own office, negotiating dates, moving in, picking out then decorating Christmas trees, dancing poolside in the moonlight, throwing herself into his arms during a raging storm, making love in the candlelight, shining bright in a flame-red dress, playing hostess to his host, waking with her in his arms, making love in the shower, her walking away.

Each memory lashed at his soul bombarding him with emotions. Isolated for nearly a year going through surgeries, recuperation and physical therapy, he'd barely felt human when he went to Ray's party. From the first moment she'd brought him to life. He'd been intrigued, frustrated, attracted.

Good God, he'd convinced himself paw prints were her toe prints just so he could see her again.

He sank onto a bench, yanked at his tie and unbuttoned the top two buttons of his shirt so he could breathe. His phone rang. He pulled out his cell and his heart lurched. Tori.

"Hello," he rasped around a constriction in his throat.

"Garrett." It hurt to hear her saying his name. "Ray said you could use some help."

"He shouldn't have bothered you."

"It's no problem," she assured him. Now he was past his original shock, he heard the chill in her tone. "I needed to talk to you anyway. We heard from the woman who lost her earring."

"Yes, my secretary gave her your information."

"The studio is closer than our showroom, so she'd prefer to pick up the earring there if possible."

He didn't care about the frigging earring. "I'll have my secretary arrange it."

"Great. Now, where are you shopping?"

"Hollywood and Highland."

"There's a lovely day spa at the Loews Hotel adjacent to the mall. A gift certificate would be nice. They should be able to put together a basket of products to make it a delightful package."

"Excellent. Thanks for your help." He cleared his throat. "How are you?"

A pause. "Hurting."

He closed his eyes. "I'm sorry."

He wanted to say more, to see her again. But he couldn't. He might not have the strength to let her go again.

"Goodbye, Garrett." Tori ended the call and his last link with her was gone.

Garrett downshifted and within seconds the car shot to ninety-five miles an hour. He headed the car west, toward Santa Barbara and home. He'd feel more settled once he was back in his own space.

He couldn't get the last phone call out of his mind. During most of their contract he'd dealt with Tori, an unusual circumstance for By Arrangement. Lauren usually dealt with the client. But from the very beginning he'd gone straight to Tori. She'd always been warm and approachable.

Her cool tone hammered home the fact Tori didn't want to talk to him. From the way she said goodbye, he deduced By Arrangement wouldn't be accepting any more contracts with Obsidian Studios.

His chest clenched, making it hard to breathe.

Needing to get out of his head, he turned on the radio, flipped through the stations. He tried a sports station first, but couldn't find a spark of interest in who won the football play-offs, so he switched to hard rock. A few minutes later he turned the radio off with a savage twist of his wrist.

The music made his head hurt and provided no release from his revolving thoughts.

There would be no release until he successfully buried his feelings behind the armor he'd built to protect his heart.

But no matter how hard he tried, he couldn't bury the hurt this time. Tori cracked the shields with her quirky good cheer, quick creative mind and genuine caring, not just for him, who spurned most overtures, but everyone around her. She'd brought light into his life, made him feel again. He could choose to hide. Eventually shore up the shields until all feelings disappeared.

Or he could reach for the light and push the darkness out.

His heart pounded, a frantic beat, reminding him he was alive. He thought of the risk if she should reject him, and a strange sense of calm came over him. She loved him. He trusted her. Ray had said it. Garrett would be safe with her.

He checked the rearview mirror and began to make his way to the right-hand lane and the nearest off-ramp. He was turning around and going after the woman he loved.

He commanded his phone to place a call. He let out a held breath when it was answered.

"Lauren, about that third date, I need your help."

Tori pulled up to The Old Manor House with mixed feelings. She really didn't want to be here. Too many bittersweet memories. Lauren should be the one returning the earring. She'd agreed to handle the last of Obsidian Studios' business.

So of course this was the only time their client from last night could do their closing interview. Tori volunteered to meet with them, but Lauren was already on that side of town, and she assured Tori Garrett wouldn't be home while she was at the house. When they each completed their meetings, they'd get together and drive home to Palm Springs.

With any luck she wouldn't even have to get out of her car. She parked in front, in clear view of anyone coming up the drive. The temperatures had dropped overnight and the day was chilly. Heavy clouds speckled the sky. After a few minutes, the cold finally drove her inside.

This would give her a chance to return the key he'd given her while she stayed here. She'd planned to mail it to the studio. Her hand shook a little as she set it on the kitchen table. She paced the room, trying not to think of the meals she'd shared with Garrett.

She missed starting the day with him, talking to him, working with him. Him.

When her mind jumped to the night of the storm and she remembered how his body pressed hers to the sturdy table, she moved into the parlor.

She fingered the earring in her pocket. Where was the owner? The longer Tori lingered the more chance she'd run into Garrett. A glance at the mantel clock showed the woman was ten minutes late.

Nerves bristling, she walked through the downstairs rooms. In a professional capacity, of course. The cleaning crew had done a great job. Garrett had left the decorative lights lit and the place looked beautiful, festive. If she did say so herself. She turned away from the tree they'd decorated together, needing no reminders of his deprived childhood.

She heard a car pull up and breathed a sigh of relief until she saw the Maserati. Oh, no, this wasn't going to happen. She hiked her purse strap over her shoulder and went out the front door. She'd hand off the earring and be on her way.

He met her on the bottom step. Her higher position put them eye to eye. He looked more peaceful than she'd ever

seen him. Great, her heart ached with the active pain of
an abscessing tooth and he'd found the tranquility life had
denied him.

She held up the earring. "The owner is running late.
I'll be on my way now that you're here."

His hand wrapped around hers. "Can you stay for a few
minutes? I'd like to talk to you."

She shook her head, pulled her hand free. Seeing him
melted her insides. If she gave him half a chance, he'd
change her mind. And that would not be a good thing.

"I have to go. Lauren and I are leaving town this afternoon." She tried to slide past him.

He shifted to block her, the movement bringing him
closer, so his male scent reached her, setting her senses
spinning.

"A few minutes won't delay you much."

"There's really nothing more to say." She retreated a
step. Then sidestepped and went around him, making for
her car.

"I love you."

She froze. Had she heard right?

Strong hands settled on her shoulders, and his warm
breath brushed over her ear. "I love you."

She shook her head, turned to face him, arms crossed
over her chest. "No. You don't get to say that to me. You
don't believe in love."

"You showed me." He caught her hand, brought it to
his mouth. "Come inside. Let's talk. I have a Christmas
gift for you."

"No." She backed up a pace. A gift to remember him
by was the last thing she wanted. Bad enough to have a
broken heart to mark the holiday into the future. "Give it
to someone else."

"It's just for you."

"Don't, Garrett." Confused, she tugged at her hand, pushing the rising hope aside. She didn't know why he was messing with her, but she couldn't let herself believe. Leaving had been hard enough when she thought he didn't care. How much worse would it be if she gave in to her love and lost him again? "I have to go."

He held on to her. "You love me, too."

"I loved you when I walked away. Nothing has changed."

"I've changed. Give me a chance to show you."

She chewed her lip. He sounded so sincere. "Five minutes."

His face lit up. "You won't regret it. Come with me." Grabbing her hand, he led her inside and out onto the terrace.

She shivered. "Maybe we should talk inside. It's cold out here."

"We have to watch for Mrs. Davis. We'll be able to see her car come up the drive."

Avoiding his gaze, she focused on the scenery. The Christmas tree lights were on out here, too. Shiny ornaments glimmered in the fading sunshine. She rubbed her hands together.

"I'll light the fire." He led her to the fire pit. A fire had been laid and he used a fireplace lighter to get it going. Then he sat down beside her on the bench seat. "I've missed you."

"Me, too." She stared down at her hands. "It's only been two days and it feels like forever."

"Too long for me. In all the time I've stayed at the Old Manor I've never seen or heard a ghost. Now it's haunted with images of you. I can't sleep, can't think of anything but you."

"It'll fade," she whispered, "just like every good memory you've buried."

"I deserve that." He took her hand, played with her fingers. "It was easier not to feel at all, so yeah, I buried the good with the bad. It became habit after a while to focus my feelings into my films."

"That's why story is so important to you."

He inclined his head. A soft wisp of wind blew a strand of hair across her face. He reached to brush it away and she ducked her head.

White fluff began to drift past her vision. She dismissed it as something in the air until some landed on her legs and melted into the fabric of her jeans. Her head jerked up. Snowflakes floated down on the terrace.

She looked with wonder at Garrett. "It's snowing."

"Merry Christmas."

"Oh, God. Oh, Garrett." Tears added to the snow drops on her cheeks. Somehow he'd tuned in to her childhood fantasy and arranged to give it to her. She threw her arms around his neck, hugging him with all her might. "Thank you."

How did she walk away from someone who saw so clearly into her heart?

"You turned my life upside down, Tori. My somber demeanor didn't deter you at all. You were irreverent and friendly, pushy and caring. You tried to deceive and fool me, but were horrendously bad at both."

She squirmed a little. "You never said how you knew I wasn't Lauren."

"I always know when it's you," he said simply.

Okay, that got to her, too. As a twin, knowing someone saw you as you touched something deep inside, filling a void she hadn't even known she had. He was racking up points left and right, but could she trust this turn in his feelings?

"I didn't want to deceive or fool you. It was your own fault."

"Please. You manipulated me to get your way. Then you moved in. And you were dragging me out to shop for Christmas trees and conning me into decorating one. Cooking and sharing coffee in the morning. You gave me a home, Tori. You can't just take it away again."

Every memory he dragged out meant something to her, too. The house had become a home, a dream she hadn't allowed herself to believe in. Did she dare take a chance?

"Garrett, you can't just flip a switch and suddenly change. I believe you want to, but a month from now you could find it all too much and long for your isolated existence again."

"You said I'd have to address the pain that caused my behavior or be buried under the weight of it. All I know is I can't change the past. And right or wrong, I lost a lot of my anger at my father when he left me the studio. But for me what really matters is my trust in you. If you never give up on me, I promise never to give up on us."

"That's beautiful." Oh, he shamed her. She'd chided him for being afraid to risk, boasted she'd risk everything for love, and yet she'd left when he'd been reaching out. Because she feared his power over her, feared love. She knew how much it hurt to lose someone. And her feelings for Garrett were so much stronger than what she'd felt for Shane. Looking deep into Garrett's gray eyes, something eased around her heart.

Gaze locked on hers, he leaned forward and kissed her, a soft meeting of lips as his gift of snow floated around them.

Love bloomed brighter, grew stronger as walls fell. She trusted him, too. With her heart, with her future, with her soul.

"I love you," she said against his mouth.

"And you'll marry me?"

She pulled back. "Marriage? Don't you think that's moving kind of fast?"

He cupped the back of her head, dragged her close for

a demanding melding of mouths and crush of bodies. "No reason not to move fast when you're certain of something. How does a Valentine's Day wedding sound to you?"

"A wedding in less than two months?" She found it sounded good. "Luckily I know a good event company. I think we could make that happen."

He grinned his beautiful smile and lowered his head again. "I'll take that as a yes."

* * * * *

Mills & Boon® Hardback

September 2014

ROMANCE

The Housekeeper's Awakening	Sharon Kendrick
More Precious than a Crown	Carol Marinelli
Captured by the Sheikh	Kate Hewitt
A Night in the Prince's Bed	Chantelle Shaw
Damaso Claims His Heir	Annie West
Changing Constantinou's Game	Jennifer Hayward
The Ultimate Revenge	Victoria Parker
Tycoon's Temptation	Trish Morey
The Party Dare	Anne Oliver
Sleeping with the Soldier	Charlotte Phillips
All's Fair in Lust & War	Amber Page
Dressed to Thrill	Bella Frances
Interview with a Tycoon	Cara Colter
Her Boss by Arrangement	Teresa Carpenter
In Her Rival's Arms	Alison Roberts
Frozen Heart, Melting Kiss	Ellie Darkins
After One Forbidden Night...	Amber McKenzie
Dr Perfect on Her Doorstep	Lucy Clark

MEDICAL

A Secret Shared...	Marion Lennox
Flirting with the Doc of Her Dreams	Janice Lynn
The Doctor Who Made Her Love Again	Susan Carlisle
The Maverick Who Ruled Her Heart	Susan Carlisle

0814GEN STD HB

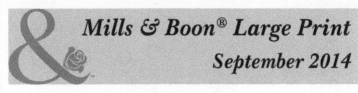

Mills & Boon® Large Print

September 2014

ROMANCE

The Only Woman to Defy Him	Carol Marinelli
Secrets of a Ruthless Tycoon	Cathy Williams
Gambling with the Crown	Lynn Raye Harris
The Forbidden Touch of Sanguardo	Julia James
One Night to Risk it All	Maisey Yates
A Clash with Cannavaro	Elizabeth Power
The Truth About De Campo	Jennifer Hayward
Expecting the Prince's Baby	Rebecca Winters
The Millionaire's Homecoming	Cara Colter
The Heir of the Castle	Scarlet Wilson
Twelve Hours of Temptation	Shoma Narayanan

HISTORICAL

Unwed and Unrepentant	Marguerite Kaye
Return of the Prodigal Gilvry	Ann Lethbridge
A Traitor's Touch	Helen Dickson
Yield to the Highlander	Terri Brisbin
Return of the Viking Warrior	Michelle Styles

MEDICAL

Waves of Temptation	Marion Lennox
Risk of a Lifetime	Caroline Anderson
To Play with Fire	Tina Beckett
The Dangers of Dating Dr Carvalho	Tina Beckett
Uncovering Her Secrets	Amalie Berlin
Unlocking the Doctor's Heart	Susanne Hampton

Mills & Boon® Hardback
October 2014

ROMANCE

An Heiress for His Empire	Lucy Monroe
His for a Price	Caitlin Crews
Commanded by the Sheikh	Kate Hewitt
The Valquez Bride	Melanie Milburne
The Uncompromising Italian	Cathy Williams
Prince Hafiz's Only Vice	Susanna Carr
A Deal Before the Altar	Rachael Thomas
Rival's Challenge	Abby Green
The Party Starts at Midnight	Lucy King
Your Bed or Mine?	Joss Wood
Turning the Good Girl Bad	Avril Tremayne
Breaking the Bro Code	Stefanie London
The Billionaire in Disguise	Soraya Lane
The Unexpected Honeymoon	Barbara Wallace
A Princess by Christmas	Jennifer Faye
His Reluctant Cinderella	Jessica Gilmore
One More Night with Her Desert Prince...	Jennifer Taylor
From Fling to Forever	Avril Tremayne

MEDICAL

It Started with No Strings...	Kate Hardy
Flirting with Dr Off-Limits	Robin Gianna
Dare She Date Again?	Amy Ruttan
The Surgeon's Christmas Wish	Annie O'Neil

Mills & Boon® Large Print
October 2014

ROMANCE

Ravelli's Defiant Bride	Lynne Graham
When Da Silva Breaks the Rules	Abby Green
The Heartbreaker Prince	Kim Lawrence
The Man She Can't Forget	Maggie Cox
A Question of Honour	Kate Walker
What the Greek Can't Resist	Maya Blake
An Heir to Bind Them	Dani Collins
Becoming the Prince's Wife	Rebecca Winters
Nine Months to Change His Life	Marion Lennox
Taming Her Italian Boss	Fiona Harper
Summer with the Millionaire	Jessica Gilmore

HISTORICAL

Scars of Betrayal	Sophia James
Scandal's Virgin	Louise Allen
An Ideal Companion	Anne Ashley
Surrender to the Viking	Joanna Fulford
No Place for an Angel	Gail Whitiker

MEDICAL

200 Harley Street: Surgeon in a Tux	Carol Marinelli
200 Harley Street: Girl from the Red Carpet	Scarlet Wilson
Flirting with the Socialite Doc	Melanie Milburne
His Diamond Like No Other	Lucy Clark
The Last Temptation of Dr Dalton	Robin Gianna
Resisting Her Rebel Hero	Lucy Ryder

MILLS & BOON®

Why shop at millsandboon.co.uk?

Each year, thousands of romance readers find their perfect read at millsandboon.co.uk. That's because we're passionate about bringing you the very best romantic fiction. Here are some of the advantages of shopping at www.millsandboon.co.uk:

✳ **Get new books first**—you'll be able to buy your favourite books one month before they hit the shops

✳ **Get exclusive discounts**—you'll also be able to buy our specially created monthly collections, with up to 50% off the RRP

✳ **Find your favourite authors**—latest news, interviews and new releases for all your favourite authors and series on our website, plus ideas for what to try next

✳ **Join in**—once you've bought your favourite books, don't forget to register with us to rate, review and join in the discussions

Visit **www.millsandboon.co.uk**
for all this and more today!